Reveal Me

Copyright

Reveal Me

the STEELE BROTHERS series
book 5

JENNIFER PROBST

Praise for the Steele Brother Series

"Sweet and incredibly hot, you'll want to grab this bright and richly decadent fantasy come to life." -- NYT Bestselling Author, Kendall Ryan

"A great quick erotica read--it has shown how versatile she can be as an author." --Hannah's Words

"These characters have a connection that is so magnetic and genuine — you will find yourself falling at the same time they are." The Literary Gossip Book Blog

"Catch Me by Jennifer Probst is a quick, hot sexy erotic second chance romance. As always, Ms. Probst reels you in with her sensual and touching story-line." --Four Chicks Flipping Pages

"Jennifer Probst never fails to deliver sweet and sultry, heartfelt and deep. Her magical way with words bring the characters completely to life and I 'felt' rather than read her story."--Pepper Winters, NYT and USA Today Bestselling Author

"Jennifer Probst builds believably kinky characters and puts them into a situation so hot and fraught with sexual tension I had to cross my legs. Rome is a Dominant God and Sloane is a feisty yet submissive match for him." Christine D Reiss - USA Today Bestselling author of the Submission Series

"Beg Me is a wonderful mix of sexy and sweet. Hot loving and a wonderful second chance story line make for an amazing story. I devoured Beg Me in one sitting. Rem and Cara steam up the pages, but it's their love story that really kept me hooked. Open and honest, everyone can relate to these characters." Lexi Blake, NY Times and USA Today Bestselling Author

Dedication

For Jen Talty. Thank you for your friendship, feedback, and saving my ass when I need it. Love you, babe.

And for my amazing Probst Posse team. I put out the call for help and you answered. Thank you for loving and supporting my books no matter what the genre, and helping me make them better. I have the best fans and friends in the world! I'm always open to new members so if you are enjoying my work, join my group here:

https://www.facebook.com/groups/probstpossestreetteam/?ref=bookmarks

Smooches-- Jen

Dear Readers,

I loved writing this erotic, BDSM novella, but many of my loyal readers have come to expect a sexy, humorous contemporary romance filled with cute dogs, witty banter, amazing sensual tension, and some open door, arousing sex scenes.

This book is different.

The scenes are BDSM heavy. It isn't a light, funny type of book, so please be warned. I'd hate to lose my readers by having them expecting a brand that is not represented with the Steele Brother series.

Thank you, as usual, for reading.

A Special Note

I'm thrilled to announce *Reveal Me* is part of a Special Cross-Over Release with Laura Kaye's *Theirs to Take* from her Blasphemy Series!

Two of your favorite authors!

Two scorching hot erotic romance series!

Two erotic worlds collide in Reveal Me and Theirs to Take!

And the best part, you can enter both worlds right here!

Chapter One

LEONARDO SINCLAIR STEPPED into the cool darkness and swept his gaze over the soaring, vaulted ceiling of the converted church. Colorful frescoes decorated the walls and thick marble columns lined the open area. Massive stained-glass windows offered protection from the curious gazes and judgments of the outside world. A smile touched his lips as he took a deep breath. Damn, it'd been a long time since he indulged in his favorite vices.

Good thing he'd come to Blasphemy for play rather than forgiveness for his many sins. The popular Baltimore BDSM club was everything he'd hoped it would be, and he intended to enjoy every moment before it was time to head to Vegas.

Adjusting the plain black mask he wore, he moved forward, appreciating the large circular bar made of gleaming marble and the intimate set up of leather couches, chairs, and private nooks where couples gathered to chat and play. The sexy timbers of hip-hop ground out from the speakers and urged crowds onto the dance floor. He savored the scents of musk, sweat, and sex drifting in the air, heading toward the bar. He usually hated themed parties such as a masquerade ball, but when one of his brothers from his Navy days asked him to do something, he did it. So, when Jonathan and Cruz had invited him to the party before he put the East Coast behind him, he'd agreed.

Now, he was glad. The muscles in his neck and shoulders softened from the long car drive. He'd grab a drink, try to find his buddies, and play with a sweet subbie tonight. Someone easy and experienced. Someone he'd enjoy for a few hours in mutual satisfaction and never look back on. Someone—

"About time you got here," the familiar voice called out.

He turned around with a grin, shaking his head at the wolf mask covering the top half of Jonathan's face. "Got stuck in traffic. Please don't tell me I'm supposed to be channeling some sort of animal here?"

"Like an ass? Nah, you're good. Let's just say I'm in the mood to hunt tonight."

Leo laughed and they embraced. Jonathan's quick wit and humor made for an easy friendship, but it was his fierce loyalty and work ethic that earned Leo's respect. With his staggering height and long blonde hair, he had a quiet presence that screamed authority. "Is there a particular target you have in mind?" Leo asked. "Or is it an open field?"

Jonathan's gaze narrowed thoughtfully. "Oh, there's a target. Her name is Hartley. Tonight's her first time at Blasphemy."

"Sounds promising. Cruz on board?"

"You better believe it," another voice said from his left. Leo turned, recognizing Cruz's short, dark hair and tattoos over warm brown skin even beneath the smooth, famously carved white mask. Shorter than Jonathan, Cruz had bulging muscles that either had a woman running in fear or begging for more. They clapped shoulders, and a fierce wave of emotion clipped through him. He'd forgotten how much he missed his friends. It had been too long.

Leo raised his brow. "Are you supposed to be the lamb to his wolf?"

Cruz winked. "Wouldn't you like to know? Besides, gotta keep her guessing. Much more fun that way, as you've told us many times."

They all laughed. Leo waved his hand in the air. "This is amazing. I can't believe you're both part owners of this place."

"We'll introduce you to the other Masters later," Cruz said. "Now that we have the boat building and restoration business under control, we're able to enjoy ourselves a bit more. The people at Blasphemy have become a second family to us."

"I'm glad, you deserve it." After the Navy, they'd all struggled with finding the right fit and place to settle down. The military seemed the only thing that could temporarily satisfy his innate restlessness— always pushing him toward the next adventure. It was good Jonathan and Cruz seemed to find their fit here in Baltimore. Maybe he'd finally find his same place in Vegas. God knows, his cousins had been on his ass for years to go out and join them.

Cruz motioned him over. "Come on, I'll get you a whisky and we'll show you around."

"Sounds good."

They moved past the dance floor and deeper into the club, unveiling specialized theme rooms that catered to every dark, delicious whim, and a beautiful high platformed stage for various demonstrations. Leo crossed his arms and watched a willowy blonde floating above her Dom, her naked body bound with intricate rope work that offered her up like an artistic sacrifice. Low moans broke from her lips, and her body shook and shivered under her Dom's flick of the whip.

The crowd surrounding them was respectfully silent, yet caught up in the sensual tension ready to explode before them. Leo enjoyed the tight feel of skin over his bones, and the low punch of heat in his gut that preceded the anticipation of mastering an open, willing female. He'd always known he needed more in his sexual relationships, even young. The deep satisfaction of pleasuring another, of stripping away the walls and bullshit to get to the core—to become truly free with another—that's what kept him coming back to BDSM.

"Your wristband marks you as an experienced Dominant," Jonathan said, walking back toward the bar section. "All the subs have color coded bands that mark their limits and experience level. You're free to roam and pick from the crowd and all rooms are available for your use—we've approved you for full access. We're using the masquerade theme to build membership, encourage more of the newbies to participate, and hopefully push some soft limits. Masks must stay on at all times. It's up to the individuals at the end of the session if they want to exchange true identities."

"Thanks. Honestly? This is one of the nicest clubs I've seen. You two have done good."

Jonathan nodded, pride shining in his eyes through the mask. "You still have to head out tomorrow?" he asked. "We were hoping you could stay with us for a few days."

"Appreciate it, but the new job starts and I want to get settled in."

"No better place than Vegas to bust some criminals. Who would've thought a math nerd could be so in demand for gambling?" Cruz smirked.

Leo laughed. "It was either DC or Sin City. Guess which one is a better fit?" His math talent had started young, and he'd learned early he could make buckets of money by gambling. Until he got busted by the casino's highly-paid security boss. Instead of a hospital visit or getting black balled, they offered him a job in Atlantic City. It fit his needs for a while until the restlessness hit again, and he enlisted in the Navy. His cousins were all poker dealers settled in Vegas, and had already set him up with a job. The idea of being around family called to him. He'd been alone for too many years, relying on his service buddies, but he missed his cousins and felt ready to stay in one place for a while.

Jonathan gave a mock shudder. "It may be good for sin, but I wouldn't be caught dead in the desert. No water, no beach, and no boats. Sounds like the devil's terrain to me."

Cruz rolled his eyes. "You can take the surfer dude out of California, but you can't take California out of the man."

Leo chuckled. "I get it. But the pay is good, the air conditioning is cold, and the women are hot. Plus, I need a new challenge. The casino has been getting jacked lately and they think I can make the bust. Could be fun."

"No doubt you'll do it. And if you get bored, you always have a place here," Jonathan said, slapping him on the back.

He nodded. "That means a lot."

"Any idea what type of submissive you're looking for tonight?" Cruz asked.

"Been a while since I've indulged," he admitted. "I'm open to all possibilities, as long as the woman understands it's one night with no strings."

"Good, cause we'd like to introduce you to someone. Someone we think you'd enjoy," Cruz said. The man's dark eyes practically glinted with conspiracy and the zeal of a set-up. Cruz had always had a hidden soft side underneath that hard-assed demeanor.

"Trying to play matchmaker?" He cocked his head and studied his friends. "Or keeping me away from your sweet thing so she doesn't fall for me and dump you two?"

Cruz snorted. "Dream on."

Jonathan grinned. "She's a friend of Hartley's. I'd like to hook her up with someone I can trust. She's newer to the lifestyle. Only been a member for the past few months and hasn't played often. I think you'd get along."

Leo considered, then shrugged. His friends knew his tastes well, and though he usually preferred experienced subs, introducing a newbie into his world was always a fun challenge. "Sure."

Cruz and Jonathan exchanged a satisfied look. Interesting. His friends weren't the matchmaking types.

He wondered if this Hartley was the cause, and hoped it was. They both deserved happiness. They'd gone to the Naval Academy together, were partners in the boat building business, and liked to share women. It was hard to settle down with a woman who'd be a good match for both of them, and open to a ménage situation.

God knows, he couldn't find that type of connection, and he was only one Dom, not two.

Jonathan's gaze sharpened past his right shoulder and a slow smile tugged his lips. "Speak of the devil," he murmured. "Here she comes."

Leo turned. Then froze.

Holy shit.

He'd been an experienced Dom for almost a decade, and not once had he felt the earth beneath his feet shift. He was known for his control and tight rein on his emotions. He didn't believe in star-struck first love, gazes meeting across a crowded room, or anything that stunk of sugar spun romance that held no depth.

Until now.

His damn tongue stuck to the roof of his mouth. Were his eyes bugging out like a horn dog pre-teen? If his reaction hadn't been so surprising, he'd be humiliated. First impressions were critical during an initial Dom and Sub meet, and he'd just committed a newbie mistake. Staring at her like a love-struck school boy gave her the upper hand. Fuck—he'd never live this down.

"Leo, this is Hartley Farren, and her friend Scarlett Rose. Ladies, you may address Leo as Sir since he is not a Blasphemy Master."

They gave him a respectful nod, Hartley in an intricately patterned soft black mask that covered her eyes and nose and extended down unevenly over her cheeks. It almost appeared more tattoo than lace. And Scarlett in a more traditional sparkling black-and-red cut-out mask that made her eyes appear huge.

Still unable to communicate, he concentrated on Hartley and tried to get his shit together. Hartley smiled sweetly, a nice blush of color on her cheeks as she greeted him. Her sideswipe look at Jonathan and Cruz told him everything he needed to know. The little subbie was just as intoxicated with his friends as they were for her. He managed to murmur a greeting and say a quick prayer of thanks Hartley wasn't the one who had him tongue-tied. No, it was the woman standing quietly at her side who stole his full attention.

Everything about her seemed like a contradiction. Though she stood completely still, an intense energy pulsed from her aura, reminding him of a downed live wire, crackling in sharp, intermittent bursts. Coal black hair fell almost to her waist in wild waves, untamed and made for his fingers to fist and pull. Inky dark eyes met his gaze directly, without a shred of shyness or hesitation. Framed by lush lashes, they tilted slightly outwards like a cat, emphasizing the angled cut of the simple black mask that hid half of her face. Her lips were full, and painted in the color of her name—a bold slash of blood-red.

His gaze probed; studied; analyzed. Her outfit was pure temptation. A skimpy red slip in shiny satin. Dipping low in the front, her cleavage teased him, and the fabric clearly showed her hard nipples. Her skin was pale, smooth, and looked soft to the touch. She was all ripe curves—ass and breasts and hips, and his fingers itched to touch and hurt and soothe. It looked as if she'd been about to get dressed, then decided to go out as is. The kicker was something so simple, probably not many Doms would notice.

Her bare feet.

Most women enjoyed wearing fuck-me shoes at a club. Besides feeling sexy, it gave them a sense of power and height. He'd always been more turned on by the vulnerability and bravery of no shoes. If she was indeed new to BDSM, her choice indicated an almost rebellious courage that stiffened his cock and sped up his heart rate.

How long had it been since a woman struck him speechless?

Never.

His continued silence must have urged her to speak. "It's nice to meet you, Sir," she said. Her words were slow and deliberate, with a husky smokiness that curled at the edges. Damned if he couldn't wait to hear her beg him in that delicious voice.

Finally, words sprung free from his throat. "The pleasure's mine. I hear we're both new to Blasphemy."

"Yes, Sir. I joined two months ago," Scarlett said, her eyes still on him. Right where he wanted them.

"And what about you, Hartley?" he asked with a smile.

"Scarlett spoke so highly of the club, she helped convince me to give it a try," Hartley said, chewing her bottom lip. "Now I'm just hoping I don't mess anything up."

Jonathan took her hand. "You're not doubting that we'll guide you every step of the way, are you?"

"Oh, no. I mean, no, Sir," she said.

"Maybe we need to show her exactly what that means," Cruz said, his voice full of dark, sensual promise.

Jonathan nodded and tugged Hartley between them. "Mmm, maybe we do."

Leo studied Scarlett. She seemed amused by the interaction, not fretful, which told him she was comfortable enough to know Cruz and Jonathan would never hurt Hartley.

"Come with us, little one," Cruz commanded. "It's time for your first lesson."

"Lesson?" Hartley asked, dark eyes going wide.

Jonathan flanked her other side, guiding them away. "No speaking unless asked a direct question. Leo, Scarlett, I'll check in with you later. Have fun."

His friends left them alone amidst the squeak of leather and hiss of whip; the grinding music and clink of glasses; the smell of sex and sweat hanging thickly in the air.

Leo waited. He figured she'd either chatter, step back nervously, or dive right in with questions. And once again, she surprised him.

She said nothing.

Those Gypsy eyes stared back, not with challenge, but with patience. Waiting for him to lead. Waiting for him to speak first. She may be a newbie, but Scarlett had already pleased him faster than some of the more experienced women he'd played with in the past.

Oh, he was going to enjoy the evening very much.

"I'd like us to get to know one another before we discuss play. Would you like to go talk?" He offered his hand with an invitation she was completely free to decline.

Her gaze assessed him. He watched the thoughts flicker across her face, noting she had a mind that preferred logic to emotion. Fact and figures trumped impulse. He'd spent years in the lifestyle studying women and their thought patterns, finding how each unique personality needed a particular type of play for maximum effect. He'd begun to wonder if the scientific game of figuring them out had become more important than the physical aspect. Damn depressing, but this woman had already pushed his buttons without saying anything. Perhaps, there was something more here.

She reached out and took his hand, allowing him to lead her to the private area away from the main activity of the club. He chose a room that reminded him of a library, comfortable with the dark leather chairs, thick burgundy carpeting, and bookshelves filling up the far wall. An antique light burned low on the desk, wrapping them in dark intimacy. The room was perfect for playing naughty secretary, and the quick image of her sprawled on the desk, her bare bottom lifted for the slap of his hand, burned his vision.

She lowered herself onto the sofa, the short hem of her slip hiking up past her thighs. Her skin was pale and smooth. He couldn't wait to see the contrast of his darker skin against hers, sliding in between those gorgeous plump thighs to pleasure her.

As if she caught his thought, her breath hitched, so low he barely heard. Her fingers tugged the hem down in a display of nerves, before settling back into her quiet intensity.

Yes. This woman would be fun to watch shatter. Now he needed to find out how deep her control really went.

"I'd like to begin with some questions. I ask them so I can get all the important information to decide what you're looking for and what you need tonight."

"Don't you believe I already know what I need?"

Her voice reminded him of classic Lauren Bacall—growly, sexy, and deep. Already, her intellectual challenge told him her brain was usually in control of her body. His favorite type of woman to play with. "No. Many times a sub thinks she knows, but her Dom sees something more. How much do you know about BDSM?"

"I started with research from books and the Internet. Then I took the orientation at Blasphemy. I've been a member for a few months."

Good, at least she had some hands-on experience. He'd met way too many women turned on by erotic romance and diving into the club scene without realizing what was fact and what was fiction. Safety was always priority number one.

"Have you scened often?"

She stiffened. "No. Just twice."

His brow quirked. "Why?"

She considered him before giving an answer. Beneath her inexperience lay a touch of a brat—one of his favorite types. She seemed to naturally want to challenge a Dom. He'd need to use a firm hand. "I didn't really connect with the Doms."

Interest piqued. "Did they push too hard? Force you to say your safe word?"

She shook her head. "No, the opposite. I was frustrated after the session. During my orientation, I dealt with the Masters which I found more satisfying."

Hmm, she probably played with newer dominants and couldn't forge a connection. "Did you try to communicate your frustration to them? Tell them what you wanted from the experience?"

"It wasn't their fault they couldn't get me off."

Interesting. Her tone held a touch of hostility, contradicting her words. There was something deeper going on and he intended to figure it out. "Some matches don't work out, just like in the vanilla world. Your Dom is responsible for giving you pleasure, and it's not your fault if you weren't satisfied. Unless, of course, you kept something important from him. Was that the case?"

She shook her head.

"Then we'll need to remedy that experience."

She nodded, but he glimpsed the flare of doubt in her dark eyes. He lowered his voice in warning. "Since you are aware of the club rules, I'll expect to hear 'Yes or No Sir' or we'll need to begin our session with punishment."

Those red lips opened in a tiny O, then snapped close. "Yes, Sir."

"What do you do, Scarlett?"

"I'm a statistician. I've worked for the government the past five years but I'm moving to the private sector."

His interest peaked. A math nerd and a submissive. A heady combination. He, too, loved the calming effect of numbers and solving the puzzles they offered to understand the world. It was hard finding people who became passionate about the beauty of mixing simplicity with complexity through math. He bet she had issues shutting off that powerful mind and concentrating on her body. He made a mental note.

"I notice you haven't checked off many hard limits for a beginner." Her bracelets clearly showed she was open to pretty much anything, including sex. "You're open to pain. Flogger, spanking, cane, whip? Preferences?"

"I was told while I experimented with my threshold I could always use the club's safe word— red—or yellow, to slow down."

He nodded, pleased. "Correct. Since we're only playing tonight, I'll concentrate on core basics rather than testing limits. That's for your future Dom to decide during your training. Do you agree?"

"Yes, Sir."

"And sex is on the table?"

Not even a slight blush marred her pale cheek. "Yes, Sir."

His cock twitched. He tamped down on his arousal and concentrated on the conversation. Plenty of time for his little head later. "Tell me about your background. I'd like to make sure you have no triggers."

"I don't." He arched his brow in warning. "I mean, I don't, Sir."

"It wasn't a question, Scarlett. I never go into a play session without feeling comfortable about my sub. This is for safety—for both of us."

Her chin tilted up slightly. Definitely defensive. Definitely a secret there he was dying to probe. "I'm divorced. It became a bit rocky at the end, but it's been a year now so I've worked through it. I went to therapy, so you won't have any surprises."

Admiration cut through him. He always believed everyone should get counseling just to get through life's pitfalls but it took guts to ask for help. "I'm sorry. Did you engage in BDSM play with your husband?"

"No, Sir."

She didn't seem to want to expand, so he pushed further. "Light bondage? Blindfold? Role play? Anything?"

"No, Sir."

Her stark admission told him more than he needed. Though he wanted more, he was pretty damn sure her ex hadn't been into bedroom kink and it had eventually become a problem. He studied her stiff body and distant eyes. No, this wasn't the way to go into their first session. She needed to be open to the experience or he'd be fighting ghosts he wasn't sure of. Going with his gut, he dove for the jugular.

"Little one, I understand it's hard to spill your innermost stuff to someone who's a stranger, but in under an hour, you're going to be naked, wet, and coming on my tongue. We could do this the hard way, or the easy way. The more I know about what you want and are looking for tonight, the better it will be. Use the mask as a tool to allow yourself to take the leap. But also know, I will strip away not only your clothes, but all those walls you've built to protect yourself. Now, make your decision."

Shock flared in her dark eyes, before quickly becoming masked. But she didn't duck her chin or try to hide. He watched her mentally step back and recalculate. Leo didn't know if she was ready to dive deep yet, but he sensed if he didn't push, they both may regret it later. Sex wasn't just an orgasm or feeling good for a few minutes. It was the biggest mind fuck of all—because it started with the brain, and who a person was at the very core. The right type of sex took all that mess, twisted it up, and released it hard and fast, like the crack of a champagne cork. Afterward, both body and mind were cleaner. Quieter. Saner.

And that type of sex could never be boring.

Especially with this woman.

But he'd pushed harder than with others, and could have blown the whole damn thing. If she was an intellectual, she may not be able to let herself take the leap and tell him. Maybe he'd—

"I was married for three years to a man who slowly eroded everything I originally liked about myself."

Leo stilled. She spoke with a steady calm, but he caught the slight tremor in her body. Moving on pure instinct, he tangled his fingers with hers, offering her warmth, squeezing slightly in comfort. Damned if she wasn't tearing down every preconceived notion about what she'd be able to handle. This type of raw truth was rare this early on, and he'd make damn sure she felt supported. "Tell me about it, little one."

Her fingers squeezed back, accepting his offering. "I didn't think it was wrong to want more out of sex. Oh, sure, we started with vanilla, which was fine, but after the first year, I realized I craved other things. Dirty things. When I brought it up, he was shocked. Began telling me I was messed up to ask him to spank me, or tie me up. I tried to let it go, but my need kept getting worse. I tried talking to him. Asked him to experiment."

"He didn't want to?"

She shook her head. "Over time, I had to fake my arousal, but he could tell. I think it made him feel like less of a man, and he started taking it out on me. First, it was my weight. I was too big, not sexy enough for him to want me. Called me fat and useless. Then it poured out in all aspects of our life together. From how I did my job, to how I cleaned the house, and everything in between. I was a failure of a wife. I was a failure at turning him on. It went on and on. And finally, one day I realized I didn't even know who I was anymore. I looked in the mirror and saw nothing. Or at least, nothing I liked."

Anger thrummed in his veins, heating his blood. Oh, if he could bash her ex's face in, he'd be over the fucking moon. Typical shit. His ego got threatened so he took it out on his wife. "Sounds like you were strong enough to realize he has a serious condition."

She cocked her head. Coal-black waves spilled over her right cheek and tumbled over her shoulder. The scent of citrus drifted to his nostrils. Clean. Tangy. Sharp. Like her. "Condition?" she asked.

"Yeah, your ex is a true asshole." He relished her smile, then leaned into her space. The air between them crackled to life, twisting tight with a delicious sexual tension that couldn't be forced. Oh, his hands itched to get all over those gorgeous curves and show her how sexy they were. "Damned if you haven't impressed the hell out of me, Scarlett Rose. First, you were strong enough not to let him win. To claim who you were and walk away. Second, you were brave enough to tell me the truth. That's a woman I want to be with. A woman I want to give excruciating pleasure to with my mouth and tongue and teeth. Tie her up with her thighs spread wide and fuck her till she begs for mercy. Spank her ass till she's dripping wet and hot." Her pupils dilated at his words. "Would you like that?"

"Yes, Sir." This time, her words came out ragged. He raked his glance over her tight nipples, and noted her rapidly racing pulse. Citrus mingled with the musky smell of arousal. She liked the dirty talk. Good, cause so did he.

"Then our play will begin. Call me Sir at all times. Use the word yellow to slow things down. Red if you want things to stop completely."

"Yes, Sir."

"Don't be afraid to use it. Gaze lowered as I lead you to our room. No speaking unless spoken to." He studied her lush body, allowing a slight smile to rest on his lips. He hadn't looked this forward to a session in too long.

"Shall we begin?"

Chapter Two

HOLY CRAP.

This was really happening.

Scarlett tried not to shake as she followed him through the writhing crowd on the dance floor, down the long hallway, and deeper into Blasphemy. The thrum of the music and chatter dimmed, until just the teasing flick of a whip drifted from various doors, along with low groans and grunts sounding like both pain and pleasure.

Excitement flicked her nerve endings. Already, the anticipation of what could happen tightened her nipples and gave her that roller coaster feeling in her tummy. All those years of trying to ignore her darker desires sprang up and practically screamed for release. She was going to have sex with a stranger tonight. A stranger who'd bring her to orgasm by doing things to her she'd only dreamed about. A stranger hidden behind a simple black mask, but who burned with an inner fire that both aroused and terrified her.

She kept her gaze demurely lowered, but his image had already imprinted on her brain. When Hartley had mentioned Jonathan and Cruz wanted her to meet their Navy friend, she'd been hesitant. Her first official sessions at Blasphemy had been disappointing. She'd been hoping to meet a Dom who knew exactly how to arouse her, but the moment she'd gotten naked, those damn negative voices flared. The harder she'd tried to ignore them, the worse they got, and instead of getting wet when he'd put his hands on her, she'd gotten stiffer and more miserable.

The second time, she requested the flogger, hoping that would give her the push needed to get out of her head. She'd liked it, but didn't achieve anything close to orgasm, so she'd figured maybe it wasn't for her.

But tonight, she had her mask. She'd finally feel safe enough to push her limits. Her fantasies revolved around submitting to a man she'd never see or hear about again. Since Leo was both experienced and trustworthy, Scarlett figured he'd be perfect to help her. She'd only be in Baltimore for a few more nights before heading to Vegas. This was her last shot to experiment at Blasphemy before she moved.

Though, she had a sinking feeling Leonardo Sinclair would not be a man easily forgotten.

From his sinful black hair, sexy stubble, and rock-hard body, he was a man who ate up the space in a room, and owned it. Simply dressed in black pants and a black t-shirt, he shimmered with trapped, animal like energy. The way he regarded her in utter stillness caused goosebumps to prickle her skin. That hooded, dark gaze traveled every inch of her body, probing her gaze behind his mask with such punch, Scarlett was terrified he already knew every one of her secrets.

Corded arms held intricate tattoos in artistic beauty. She loved tats, but had never dated a man with one. It took discipline not to reach out to trail a finger over the gorgeous designs and ask a dozen questions. Of course, that action would have gotten her punished.

Oh, my, what would it be like to have this man punish her?

When he sat and spoke with her, the warmth of his hands had surprised and comforted her. Though he seemed deliberate with every movement, he was quick to offer touch, which had immediately softened her. How did he seem to know what she needed when they'd only met? Was it because he was a practiced Dom? Or was it this particular man?

The questions danced in her mind with every step toward the play room. Scarlett snuck a quick peek at his tight ass, framed perfectly in those neatly pressed pants. He was easily over six two, and seemed to automatically part the crowds ahead of him like Moses and the Red Sea. He walked like a man who knew exactly what he wanted and had no doubts he'd achieve it. The sheer boldness of his confidence made her immediately wet, until she felt the damp lace of her panties cling to her inner thighs.

God, he hadn't even touched her yet. She hadn't been this wet in so long, she feared some of her erogenous parts had been broken. Looks like they only needed a good lube.

She tamped down on the ridiculous thought, fighting back a nervous giggle that was completely foreign to her, and entered the farthest room on the right. She blinked against the sudden darkness, tensing only slightly as he shut the door with a soft click behind her.

Relief flooded through her veins. He'd chosen one of the simplest rooms in the club. There were no hard-core themes, which may make things easier. She'd refused to mark limits with her bands. She'd been locked up for so long in a sexual prison, Scarlett hated to reject anything, even if it scared her. Now she just had to hope her courage didn't fail.

Her gaze travelled over the giant St. Andrew's cross and beautiful red cabinct that held an array of floggers, nipple clamps, vibrators, and other toys. The four-poster king size bed was dressed in earth and burgundy tones, with thick blankets and fluffy pillows. The walls were covered in red velvet, wrapping them in a sound proof haven. Somehow, the simplicity lent to an air of intimacy the other more elaborate rooms lacked.

Leo moved in front of her, and she focused on his shiny black shoes.

"You may look up."

His voice was like gravel mixed with sand—rough, gritty, earthy. She fought a shiver and stared back at him.

"I have an important question."

She tilted her head, curious. "Yes, Sir?"

"Did you look up at any time during our walk here?"

Crap. She blinked, taking a moment to sift through her options. Then fell back on truth. "Yes, Sir."

Had his lip twitched slightly or was it her imagination? "Why?"

Her cheeks warmed. "Because I was staring at your ass."

This time, she caught the curl of his lower lip. "Such a bad girl for disobeying." He clucked, reaching out to tug her long hair, moving his fingers through the thick strands, rearranging them over her breasts. "Such a good girl for telling me the truth." Still stroking, he let his hands coast over her straining nipples, brushing lightly against the satin fabric so the delicious sensation streamed through her blood, turning to liquid heat. She tried to keep still, but the teasing rhythm continued until her body arched for more. He murmured under his breath, then those gentle fingers grasped her nipple and twisted. The sudden bite of pain hit, then shimmered into a strange aching pleasure, wringing out a gasp. His voice held a dark satisfaction. "I'll decide whether to punish or reward you in a bit. For now, take off your clothes."

He stepped back a few inches and crossed his arms. The sudden distance reminded her he was in charge, and the thought softened her muscles. She just had to obey. If she kept that mantra in mind, she'd do fine.

Lifting her chin, she slowly lowered the straps down off her shoulders and let the blood-red satin fall to her feet. Trying to remain graceful, she bent and scooped up the skimpy slip, folding it neatly. Her red lace thong was brand new. She'd waxed herself clean and indulged in a seaweed wrap so her skin was smooth and polished. Excitement and shame mixed in a heady cocktail, dampening her underwear.

"Beautiful. Now the rest, and hand them both to me."

Swallowing, reminding herself she was safe behind her mask, Scarlett dragged the thong over her hips and stepped out of it, then handed them over with a trembling hand. He brought the fabric up to his nose and took a deep breath. "You're very wet." Her ex would've found fault with such arousal but Leo's dark eyes glinted with satisfaction. "Does this excite you? Standing in front of me naked while I'm still fully dressed?"

She swayed slightly but held his gaze. "Yes."

"Good. I want you to spread your legs as wide as possible and interlace your fingers behind your head. I'm going to examine you. You can keep your gaze on me."

She refused to bite her lip in weakness—absolutely refused. It was so damn cliché. Grinding her teeth in determination, she focused on the heat pulsing between her thighs and obeyed. The humiliation of being displayed for his pleasure should have shocked her. Instead, her mind began to fizz pleasantly, softening all those sharp voices and constant assessments that kept her continuously distracted.

He watched her while he closed the distance; his gaze an almost tangible thing as he probed every open part of her, raking from the top of her head to her red painted toes. Lingering on the hard tips of her breasts, down her belly, and to the junction between her thighs, already plump and damp. Scarlett fell into the fantasy, the sense of freedom pulsing in her veins. Finally, she was able to let go. Finally, she—

You have to shop at the fat women's store. Do you think that's sexy?

I can't even get an erection looking at you naked but you're still blaming me for our lousy sex life.

Suddenly, Peter's mocking gaze was in front of her. Suddenly, her nakedness wasn't erotic and beautiful, but something to cover up and be ashamed about. She blinked, trying to shove the image away, her arms shaking with the effort to hold the pose when all she wanted to do was duck and hide. All she saw was her ex's stare of rejection as he looked over her body. Even hidden behind her mask, she couldn't escape the shame of rejection. Her initial arousal faded. Nerves overtook that delicious sense of freedom and in that moment, she just wanted to go home.

The firm grasp on her chin yanked her back.

Leo loomed over her, a frown creasing his brow. "What happened, little one? You went somewhere that hurt you."

Shame washed over her. She'd been wrong. She wasn't ready for any of this. It was exactly what had happened the last two times. Now, Leo would blame himself for not being able to arouse her. God, she didn't blame him. How many times had she worked on her self-worth in therapy, beginning to accept who she was –physically and mentally and emotionally— intent on never making apologies again. But the first time she stood naked in the club, her old fears reared up, crippling her. He didn't want someone with these sort of hang ups, especially for one night.

It took everything she had not to duck her head in humiliation. "I'm sorry, Sir."

His frown deepened. "For what? Tell me the exact thought you had right now. Don't think—just tell me."

"I'm too fat and probably won't please you."

Mingled shock and fierce rage blasted from his eyes. His grip tightened on her chin. He leaned forward so his lips were inches from hers. He uttered each word with deliberate softness contradictory to the fierceness of his gaze. "Did you say you were fat?"

"Yes," she said miserably. She'd failed. The moment she tried to bare herself, the past roared back and crippled her confidence, even behind her mask. All this training and hopefulness leading up to this night dissipated like smoke.

"Who told you that?" he demanded. "Your ex?"

She gave a tiny nod, his fingers still gripping her chin. Scarlett waited for him to back away politely, and allow her to get dressed to leave.

"Are you saying yellow?" He stroked her cheek with such tenderness, she blinked in confusion. "Do you want to leave?"

The truth tumbled up from deep inside, surprising her with its brutal intensity. "I don't want to feel unwanted."

A curse blistered from his lips. He lowered his forehead and pressed it against her in a shattering intimate gesture. "God help that asshole if I ever get my hands on him," he muttered. He cupped her face beneath the edges of the mask, tilting her closer. His breath rushed warm across her lips with the clean scent of mint and the darker scent of whiskey. "Do you know how you made me feel when I first saw you? Like a schoolboy—clumsy and tripping on hormones, desperate to touch you, fuck you, please you." His lips brushed hers softly, like a whisper. "Your body is pure Eve, lush and full and tempting. You, Scarlett Rose, are sheer perfection and now I'm going to have to punish you so you never forget it."

His proclamation rung in the air the same time his mouth took hers.

The kiss was brutal. Stripped to the core of animal lust, his tongue pushed into her mouth with no finesse or gentleness, just a need to possess and claim and conquer. He plundered deep, stroking and biting, thrusting and ravaging her mouth, holding her head still so she had no choice to escape. He forced her to take all of him and surrender.

Something deep shifted within her. The kiss was savage but truthful, his fingers bruising her skin, his tongue deep in her mouth, his erection pressed hard against her thigh. In one quick movement, he cupped her ass and lifted her up, grinding her wet pussy onto his dick through the fabric of his pants. Pure need exploded within her and she rocked her hips greedily against him, trying for more, desperate to fill the aching emptiness between her thighs.

"This is what you do to me," he growled, sinking his teeth into her lower lip, then soothing with his tongue. The delicious taste of him swamped her, dragging her deeper into this wicked world of pleasure. "As your Dom for the evening, you gave your body over to me, and I will not allow you to demean either of us by calling yourself fat." He worked her over his straining dick, controlling her descent, scraping her clit just enough to keep her right on the edge. Scarlett moaned and wiggled closer, and then he slipped his index finger between her legs and plunged deep.

"You're so wet and tight. Purely fuckable. I can't wait to see you come."

He added another finger, and she began to lose control, his words and touch ripping down the barriers until nothing mattered but getting that orgasm, that damn elusive, gorgeous, looming orgasm that was about to tear her apart. A greedy moan escaped her lips, and he laughed low, curling his fingers deep and hitting the magic spot that gave off shockwaves of delight. His control was absolute, and she sensed no matter how she writhed or begged, her orgasm wouldn't come until he was good and ready. The knowledge thrilled her, breaking her up inside and emptying her mind completely. Nothing existed but him and what he could give her.

"Tell me right now—how do you feel?"

Her naked breasts bounced up and down as she writhed on his lap. The musky scent of arousal filled the room. Her legs were splayed wide open, and his fingers pumped deep into her pussy as he watched every flicker of expression on her face. Seconds before, she'd thought herself fat and ugly. Now, steeped deep in sensation, she knew this man wanted her on a level she'd never experienced—wanted not only to give her pleasure but to wring it from her body over and over again.

Her drugged eyes locked on his. Her voice came out in a throaty whisper. "I feel beautiful."

Satisfaction carved out the lines of his face. She had a sudden urge to tug off his mask and memorize the rough, craggy features that could look so fierce yet tender. "That's right. You are beautiful and fuckable and mine for tonight."

He plunged three fingers deep inside, stretching her, and when she bucked helplessly, he scraped her swollen clit with his thumb. Once. Twice. God, right there, she was going to come, she was going to—

He set her back down on the ground and stepped away.

Her breath came out in choppy gasps. Her whole body tightened and screamed for release, but she waited, knowing there was more.

A small smile rested on his lips.

"Let's try this again, shall we? Except this time, with restraints."

"But—"

His brow shot up. Swallowing back a needy groan, she fell quiet. He nodded his approval, and led her over to the leather wrapped, massive cross. Her belly slowly tumbled as he positioned her in front and began binding her wrists and ankles so she was stretched like a virgin sacrifice. Arms and legs widespread into a V, she tried instinctually to free herself but the cuffs held tight. The thrill of being restrained for anything he wanted to do shuddered through her, making her head feel fizzy.

Leo took his time, testing the space between her skin and the cuffs; double checking the attachments. "How does it feel?"

Exciting. Scary. Freeing. Intoxicating.

Her body felt flushed and alive; swollen and so sensitive, one touch to her clit would set her off. Then she realized he'd been able to quiet the chaos. Right now, she felt powerful and beautiful in her vulnerability of being exposed. Tied up to be used as he saw fit. More comfortable in her skin, the way she used to be before Peter began eroding her self-confidence. How had Leo managed to help her in such a short session?

"Good, Sir," she finally managed to answer.

"Use your safe word if you need." His gaze traveled over her naked body with obvious hunger. "Let me explain now what will happen, Scarlett. You will be punished twice. One, for insulting your body—which belongs to me. Second, for not calling me Sir. I'll keep the first one easy. All you have to do is not come. Do you understand?"

Her wobbly knees gave out, but the cross held her upright. Not come? When her entire body was screaming for release? When just a touch may set her off like a rocket?

But he was dead serious. She'd heard of Doms not allowing orgasms—but could she do it?

Yes. Because she had to. She couldn't fail. Scarlett stiffened her spine and her resolve. Her brain locked on the command given to her. "Yes, Sir."

"Good. Eyes on me the whole time."

She gulped in a deep breath, tried to lock her body into position, and swore to obey.

Chapter Three

GOD, SHE WAS FUCKING GORGEOUS.

Leo stared at her naked body displayed for his view. The stiffness was gone, along with the ghosts in those beautiful Gypsy eyes. Bound to the cross, naked body offered up to him for any wicked thing he decided, he savored every expression flickering over her beautiful face. Yes, she responded nicely to restraint. He'd wondered if her analytical brain would fight, but it seemed once her options were stripped away, it was easier for her to surrender.

He'd played with many women before, and not once had they blurted out exactly what they were thinking when asked. It was obvious Scarlett was caught in her head, but once commanded, she let go. When he asked a direct question, he got a direct answer, which combined an intriguing mix of confidence and submissiveness. Watching her fall apart on him was going to be the most fun he'd had in a long time. Poor little subbie didn't realize what was about to happen.

Because he intended for her to fail his challenge.

His dick throbbed painfully. When she shut off the doubts, she exploded in his arms with a feminine demand he intended to tame. Once redirected, all that passion would be a magnificent thing to channel and explore.

But this was only for tonight.

Leo buried the disturbing thought. He didn't want to linger on the possibility he'd never see Scarlett Rose again. In a short time, she'd dug under his skin, and he needed more time.

But for now, he'd concentrate on how far he could push her into pleasure.

He approached with slow deliberateness, tugging at her hair, smoothing his palm over her shoulder blades and up the stretched muscles of her arms, giving her occasional touches or strokes on various body parts to keep her off balance. Her breath came in choppy gasps, and her skin was damp and flushed. Her pussy was glistening, the bare folds allowing him to glimpse her hard clit and the depth of her arousal. Those hourglass hips were made for gripping and deep fucking. He kept a close study on his beautiful prey, choosing silence for now to allow her to sink into the mode of submission.

"I'm going to use you now, Scarlett. Put my fingers and tongue inside you to see if I can make you scream. Stroke and lick that pretty pussy, suck on your clit, bite your nipples, and try to get you to orgasm. But you won't, will you, little one? Because I told you not to."

There. Her reaction shuddered from her core, evident in her widened eyes and dilated pupils, the stiffening of her body in anticipation. He breathed in the spicy scent of her arousal, coated on her inner thighs. Oh, she was sweet. To be the first to watch her shatter would be a humbling experience.

"Y-yes, Sir."

"And your safe word?"

"Red, Sir."

"Very good." He began with her breasts, plumping them in his palms, enjoying the heavy weight and sway. Her nipples were cherry red, reminding him of an ice cream sundae ready to be devoured. She trembled under his touch. The chains clinked gently when she tried to pull at her bonds. "If you were mine, I'd make you go topless all the time. I'd watch your breasts bounce as you walked. Watch your nipples harden in the cool air. I'd demand full access so I could play. I think there'd be many games we'd enjoy. Ice cubes. Hot wax. Clamps. Sensation play is one of my favorites."

He plucked at the tips, experimenting with the level of pain she liked. Gradually, he increased the pressure, watching her face, enjoying the glazed look in her dark eyes behind the mask and the way her mouth fell open in a tiny little O. "I'd want to fuck these breasts. Slide my cock between them and come all over your chest while you watched."

A moan escaped her swollen, damp lips. This time he squeezed with merciless pressure, finding the limit where pain refused to meld to pleasure, then lowered his head to suck hard on her nipple. He feasted and savored the taste of her skin, the clean, citrusy scent of her body lotion. He took his time, licking and learning the texture and level of sensitivity until her nipples were engorged and gleaming wet in the light. He examined his handiwork, noting the helpless tremble in her limbs, the gentle clink of chains with each pull, the fierceness of determination on her elegant face.

"Beautiful," he whispered, trailing a finger down her rounded belly. "You're doing so well, Scarlett. Such a good girl."

"Thank you, Sir." Her voice came out husky and raw.

"What other things should I do to this body tonight? Shall I spank your pussy while you lay open to me? Clamp your nipples? Kiss your body with the tip of my flogger while I push a vibrator deep in your cunt?"

He studied the shudder that shook her; the glaze of lust in her dark pupils. Oh, yes, she liked the idea of it all. And he wanted to give it to her, but right now he needed her orgasm. Needed to watch her fall apart under his hands so he could punish her the way he really wanted.

"Yes, Sir. All of it."

"A perfect answer." He dropped a kiss on her bare shoulder. Then he did what he'd been waiting for.

He sunk to his knees.

She sucked in a breath as he began to stroke her thighs, caressing the long length of her limbs, the back of her knee, the dip of her foot. He took his time, watching her body stiffen in anticipation, and finally reached her damp inner thighs. Her needy pussy practically begged for him.

God, he had to taste her or he'd go out of his mind.

With one quick movement, he parted her lips wide, exposing her hard clit. She was swollen and wet and so damn hot, he was ready to come in his pants. She gasped out a breath and those hips began to rock, desperate for what he could give her.

"Look at me," he commanded. Her gaze snapped to his. "Watch me suck your pretty little clit and make you come. You want to come, don't you, Scarlett?"

"But I'm not allowed, Sir," she choked out.

He grinned slow. "That's right. Thank you for reminding me."

Her groan was like music drifting to his ears a moment before he opened his mouth and dove in.

She tasted like musky earth and soaring sky; of salty ocean and sweet honey. Her cries filled the air as he circled the hard nub with his tongue, alternating soft licks with sharp bites. He dove three fingers deep into her channel, rubbing with an insistent pressure she tried desperately to fight but it was a battle he'd planned for her to lose. Helpless, she writhed against his mouth for more, his name a sweet chant, and then he closed his lips over her clit and sucked hard, continuing to work her with his fingers.

She came with a violent scream. Her body shuddered with the release, jerking against him, and after he'd tasted the last drop of her essence, he got to his feet.

Slumped over, the chains held her upright. Her face was relaxed with her release, but as the knowledge began to slowly dawn, those eyes widened in panic. Leo held back his chuckle, enjoying the moment when she realized she was in big trouble.

"Did you disobey my command?" he asked, his voice a whiplash. "Did you come?"

Misery etched out the lines of her face. Her lower lip trembled. "Yes, Sir. I'm sorry."

"As am I. Now, let's try this again and perhaps you'll obey me this time."

Her pretty mouth dropped open in shock. "You're going to do it again?"

His look was harsh, and she immediately backed up. "I mean, you're going to give me another chance, Sir?" she squeaked out.

He bit back the urge to laugh. God, she was perfect. A combination of innocence and stubbornness, new to this world that had begun to seem jaded. Perhaps, he'd been with too many experienced subs, not allowing himself to experience the joy of initiating a newbie.

"Yes, Scarlett. Don't disappoint me."

He turned his back on her and walked to the bureau, taking out a bullet sized vibrator that was basic but emanated some decent power. He moved slow, making sure she saw exactly what he was about to do so she had plenty of time to prepare herself. Kneeling in front of her, he set the toy to the lowest vibration and slipped it inside her still pulsing channel. She jerked a bit as he slid past her clit, then settled as the humming vibrator slid home. Leo knew it would keep her body on alert, poised perfectly at the edge. Her face scrunched up as she seemed to get her mind ready for the battle ahead. Poor little subbie. She had no idea what was about to come.

"Comfortable?"

"Yes, Sir."

"Good. Now, let's see how you'll look with a little dressing, shall we?"

A small frown settled on her brow. He moved back to the drawer and pulled out a set of nipple clamps with red jewels attached. Definitely rubies to match those deep red lips. Leo noticed her eyes had widened when he returned, as she began to understand the game rules had been upped. He pressed a kiss to her swollen, damp lips, then lowered to suck on her nipple.

Already sensitive from his previous play, they stiffened further, allowing him to easily slide on the clamp. He notched it a few cranks for discomfort but not actual pain. He addressed the other nipple, then stood back to admire his handiwork.

Caught in his chains, the rubies dripping from her nipples glittered in the light. Her hips rolled unconsciously in time to the vibrations inside, trying to fight the normal impulse to chase her orgasm.

"You are perfect," he declared. "My gorgeous fuck-toy, ready to please me. It's time for me to play. Remember, Scarlett, you have one job. Do not come."

"Y-y-yes, Sir."

He began round two slow and easy, biting down her neck, tugging gently on the rubies so she jerked with sensation, gripping her full hips and digging his fingernails in with bruising force. She responded to every touch like she was made for his hands, her determined will to fight the pleasure at the same time she embraced it, her mind and body on a beautiful collision course he directed. Covering every inch, he sucked and licked and bit, until she trembled violently in his arms, little cries escaping her lips as she tried to hold on.

By the time he dropped to his knees, she was hanging on the edge. He moved the vibrator inside her faster, ramping up to the next level, and began to tongue her clit, circling the sensitive bud with light licks meant to tease and torture. A helpless plea ripped through the air and with a shudder, she began to fall apart.

He backed off just in time, removing his tongue from her clit and stopping the vibrator. She panted. A tiny frown of concentration creased her brows, along with an expression of frustration and relief.

Damn, she was fun to play with.

He began the whole process again. And again.

When her legs began to shake and her head tossed back and forth in agony, Leo decided it was time for her to fail. He ramped up the vibrator and closed his lips around her hard clit.

"Sir! Oh, please, I can't—"

"You can. I want you to hold on."

"Oh, God!"

He moved the vibrator faster, licked faster, and tugged hard on her right nipple clamp.

A violent scream blasted from her lips, and her body gave up and gave in, convulsing with the strength of her orgasm. He bit her clit, pumping the vibrator with ferocity, and she caught another one, jerking in the chains with the power of her release. When he'd pushed her all the way, he slowly eased the vibrator out of her soaking pussy. He rolled to his feet and studied the woman before him.

Her skin was flushed and damp with sweat. She hung limp as a ragdoll, caught in his chains, the rubies gleaming from her stiff nipples. Still hidden partly behind her mask, inky dark eyes glazed with pleasure, a small, soft smile on her lips.

"Scarlett? What did you do?" he asked, curious to see if she'd panic or was too far gone with her release to care yet.

She blinked. Roused to stare at him for a while, looking as if she searched for words that made sense. "Ooops. I did it again, Sir. I'm so sorry."

He shook his head, but couldn't help his lips from twitching. He enjoyed twisting punishment to serve his purposes, especially when giving her multiple orgasms was the most fun he'd had in months. "I'll have to find another way to punish you."

"I think so, Sir."

With his dick aching for relief, he pushed his own need aside and gave into his desire to comfort. He put the vibrator on the table for cleaning, grabbed a bottle of water, then released her bonds, rubbing her wrists and ankles until the blood began to flow back. Gathering her against his chest, he lifted her up and carried her over to the bed. She embraced him with a naturalness that made his throat tighten and a strange need churn his gut. She fit perfectly in his hold, her skin warm and damp, her head tucked under his chin, arms wrapped tight around him. Leo tugged the covers over her for warmth.

A small sigh of contentment drifted to his ears. He smiled, stroking her tangled hair back from her face, rocking her gently against him. "How do you feel, little one?"

"So, good, Sir. But sorry I disobeyed you."

He chuckled. "We'll need to work on your self-control."

"I'll do better next time, Sir."

The words hit him like a sucker punch. He wanted a next time. Did she? Could this be more than a one night between strangers? Yes, he was heading to Vegas, but maybe he could find a way to make this work if she was willing. He tucked the knowledge away, figuring later he'd broach the subject and probe a bit more.

Right now, the evening wasn't over.

"Drink some water," he commanded, unfastening the top and handing her the bottle. She drank half the bottle and he set it on the nightstand. She snuggled back into his arms sleepily, and amusement cut through him. Time to go back into Dom mode. "Are you ready, little one?"

Her breathy little sigh made his dick twitch. "Hmmm?"

"I want you to flip onto your stomach and lay yourself over my knee. It's time for your spanking. I'm going to make sure you never forget to properly address your Dom again."

She sprung up from his lap, drowsiness gone. He studied the color in her cheeks and allowed a small smile to rest on his lips.

"Sir. I still have the nipple clamps on."

His smile widened. "Yes, you do. Now, flip over and show me your sweet ass, Scarlett. Don't make me ask again."

One second passed. Another. He spotted the moment she embraced the power of surrender; the intoxication of being told exactly what to do. Within those magnificent eyes lay a fierce excitement and need to please that fed his inner hunger and need for dominance. The beauty of the puzzle pieces sliding together into a perfect fit humbled him—black and white; dark and light; pain and pleasure; Dom and Submissive.

He savored all of it and waited for the final assent.

Her gaze lowered. "Yes, Sir."

Slowly, she wriggled herself around, lay carefully over his lap, and waited.

Chapter Four

SCARLETT TRIED NOT TO SHIFT but her entire body throbbed. Arms and legs dangling awkwardly, she gripped at Leo's calves for balance, toes barely touching the floor. He adjusted her over his lap, his big hands rubbing her ass in soothing strokes. Her skin tingled in sharp anticipation, sensing this spanking would be nothing like the flogger.

Already, it was horribly intimate.

Before, she'd been restrained facing a wall, and the flogger had felt a bit impersonal. She'd enjoyed the wicked flick of pain dancing on her skin, but once again, her mind pushed out any good sensation, until she was tortured about what she looked like.

The memory made her cheeks hot. Did her ass look huge to him right now? Were her hips too wide and fleshy? Was her stomach—

Whack.

She jerked at the sting on her backside, and the quick lava flow of heat in her blood. The nipple clamps swung and delivered a firm pinch.

"I will not allow you to judge this beautiful body that belongs to me." His hands rubbed hard, squeezing the sensitive spot he'd just hit. "You will keep your attention on your Dom at all times. Do you understand?"

"Yes, Sir."

"You will count each of my slaps. After each one you will say these words. 'I am beautiful.' Do you understand?"

Humiliation leaked through her. She couldn't say that. It was silly and stupid. "Sir, I don't think—"

Whack.

Holy crap, this one was even harder. She squeezed her eyes tight and tried to sort her crazy, wild thoughts.

"Did I order you to think? No. I ordered you to count each slap and say those words. Do you want to use your safe word?"

God, this was awful. So why was she so damn wet? Her pussy throbbed with emptiness and need at the same time her bottom flamed. "No, Sir," she said miserably.

"Then we'll begin."

The next slap landed on her upper thigh. She gobbled up a breath and forced the words from her lips. "One. I am beautiful, Sir."

"Very nice."

She winced as his next strike hit dead center on her right cheek. She'd always imagined a flogger or crop could administer more pain than a Dom's hand. Now she knew different. "Two. I am beautiful, Sir."

She grit her teeth and said the words over and over, until something began to loosen inside of her. Panic loomed, but she had no time to sort it out, she was too busy counting the slaps that rained down on her sore bottom. A terrible, looming sob lodged inside her chest. Her eyes stung with unshed tears she refused to shed, and as she fought viciously, Leo never stopped, until pain and pleasure melded into a sharp, colorful wave of sensation. Her world narrowed to a pinpoint, where every sting on her ass, every jerk of her nipples, every zing to her pulsing clit swallowed her whole, pushing her toward a release just out of reach. Her body became one giant ache.

The slaps became harder. The edge loomed closer. The tears bubbled up to the surface. She choked out the words, and then his next hit broke right through her barriers, letting loose a heartfelt sob, and suddenly his fingers dove deep inside her wet pussy, twisting and pumping with ferocious force and she arched back hard in desperation and need, dangling on the razor edge of madness and terrifying, violent release.

"Come for me."

The nipple clamps jerked free.

Ferocious, wicked pain shot straight to her nipples. She screamed, writhing madly in his lap, and then he pinched her hard clit and she was coming, over and over, caught in a tidal wave of pure pleasure and ecstasy. The knot deep inside unraveled and tossed her into convulsions of raw release, but Leo held her tight, absorbing every shudder and tear that shook from her body.

With a muttered curse, he tossed her onto the bed, guiding her arms over her head and her fingers around the posts of the headboard. "Don't let go," he ground out. Her sore bottom pulsed against the soft quilt, and she kept writhing as shockwaves of pleasure zapped at her body.

In a haze, she watched him undress, revealing toasty golden skin covered in dark hair, endless carved muscles, and those beautiful tats scrolled over his corded arms. His cock was thick and powerful, jutting out with animal pride. His dark eyes gleamed with fierce intent and a hungry lust that curled her toes. She squeezed the posts hard and parted her legs wide with invitation and a submission that felt completely right.

"You're going to take all of me," he commanded in that dark, silky voice. He rolled on the condom with deliberate motions. The hint of menace thrilled her and she tilted her hips up, showing him she was eager to obey. His gaze fixed on her wet, pulsing pussy with a touch of possession. "You're going to scream my name as long as you can, and maybe then I'll let you come again. And then you're going to thank me for every orgasm I deign to give you."

"Yes, Sir." She wet her bottom lip. "Please."

He yanked her hips down and settled himself between her spread thighs. His gaze ravished every inch of her body, and then he gave a grunt, reared up, and speared her with one quick, hard thrust.

She threw her head back on the pillow. His name broke from her lips. She was split apart, his throbbing cock taking up every inch of her body, and instinctually she fought him off, but he pressed his chest against hers, pinning her down on the mattress and took her mouth in a violent kiss.

His tongue plunged as deep as his cock, leaving nothing for her to keep. He demanded it all, pushing every thought out of her head except the demand for her surrender. Slowly, her muscles relaxed and softened, opening up and accepting the burning heat of his command.

Then he moved.

Tongue and cock taking her completely. Fingers bruising her hips as he held her ruthlessly in place for each thrust. And then it was happening again, her body lit from the inside, her clit demanding more pressure as the orgasm built.

"Please, Sir, please let me come."

He raised his mouth, pupils dilating his eyes until they seemed coal black, pulling her into the consuming darkness until there was no way out. "I think you can do better than that. Beg me."

He angled his body, moving her like a rag doll until he hit the spot that shimmered with shocking pleasure. Her nipples burned in agony, and her pussy clenched around his dick, and his teeth bit her lower lip and she pleased; begged; sobbed; yelling his name over and over, desperate for release.

With a satisfied grunt, he lifted her legs up high over his shoulders and thrust deeper. His fingers rubbed her clit with firm, steady pressure and he hit that magic spot again and again until she came hard.

She heard his low shout of release and he jerked his hips wildly, spilling his seed. Eyes half-closed, she watched him fall apart. Carved lips open in pleasure, chiseled jaw clenched, he was masculine power and beauty above her. And when he collapsed on the mattress, rolling her to the side to tuck her tight against his chest, Scarlett buried her face against his damp skin and treasured the sudden, glorious silence inside her.

As if he sensed the reverence of the moment, he didn't speak. Just stroked her hair, letting her absorb his body heat and strength. For the first time, she not only felt treasured, but protected. Cared for. Those silly tears stung her eyes again, but she guessed Leo had finally shown her what she'd been desperately looking for. Not only excruciating pleasure, but the freedom in her own sexuality. As the quiet stretched between them, she wondered if she should thank him, or say something witty or—

"Close your eyes for a bit, little one. Just rest."

Scarlett smiled, and with a little sigh of contentment, obeyed.

Chapter Five

LEO GLANCED DOWN at the woman in his arms.

Her eyes were closed. Those red lips were parted and held a dreamy half smile. Her brow was smooth and relaxed, and the red and black mask emphasized the pale smoothness to her skin. His fingers itched to remove the final barrier between them and demand she give up her last piece of defense.

But he didn't have the right.

He wasn't her Dom. He was moving to Vegas. This was a brief interlude between strangers.

Then why didn't she feel like a stranger?

Why did she feel familiar? Like a whisper of a memory from the moment his mouth claimed hers? It was as if she'd imprinted herself on his very flesh in the last few hours and he wasn't sure how to handle it.

He got up from the bed quietly and walked into the bathroom to get some clean washcloths. He needed to get a grip. Yes, she'd touched something inside him he'd never experienced before. Her shattering surrender and truthfulness. Her vulnerability and strength. Her sweetness and touch of spice.

But she wasn't his.

Smothering a vicious curse, he returned to the bed and began cleaning her up. She gave a small moan as he smoothed the cloth over her inner thighs and pussy. He took the second one and wiped away the dried tears on her cheek, smoothing away the sweat drying on her skin. She practically purred beneath his touch and Leo was taken aback at the violent surge of possession that swamped him.

He wanted to be the one to guide her deeper into BDSM. To learn her. Take care of her.

He needed more damn time.

"Sir? May I ask a question?"

He smiled, returning the cloths to the bathroom and sitting on the edge of the bed. "You can call me Leo while we're out of scene."

She drowsily propped herself up on her elbow. Dark waves fell over her naked breasts, allowing just the hard tip of her cherry red nipple to peak through. Her eyes gleamed with curiosity. "How long have you been a Dom?"

"About ten years now. I always felt like something was missing for me during sex, but I had no idea what it was. My cousin, Roman, educated me in the world of BDSM. He was a dominant and when I told him about my lack of sex drive, he sensed I needed to try BDSM. The first time a woman sank to her knees in front of me, I'd never felt so complete. It was as if I finally belonged and knew who I was."

"How old are you now?"

He grinned. "Thirty-five." She looked eager to ask more, but seemed hesitant, as if it was against the rules. "Scarlett, you can ask me anything you want and

I'll answer truthfully. You have just as much right to demand from me as I do from you."

Pleasure bloomed on her face. God, she was so expressive. "Are you still in the Navy?"

"No, I got out same time as Jonathan and Cruz. I work in security now."

Her gaze touched on his arms with admiration. "Did you get your tats in the Navy?"

He absently stroked the intricate designs that marked his skin. "Yeah. Serving for those years showed me some things in the world I'd been immune to." He trailed off, but her eyes urged him to continue. His ink was extremely personal and many people didn't give a shit about the why. "My father wasn't the nicest guy in the world. We had a crappy relationship, so I did my share of teen rebellion. I became wrapped up in myself and what people could do for me. Always focused on how bad or good I felt. I was selfish."

"Most teens are," she said.

"Maybe. I decided to join the navy as a big *fuck you* to my dad, who wasn't a fan of the military. Service changed me. For the first time, I saw beyond my own world and grew up. I never wanted to forget so I got ink for each of the things I learned were important."

She leaned over, moving her fingers gently over his bicep. Her cherry red nails flashed. "This?" she asked softly.

The dragon's eye stared back at her with fierce command inked in dark blue. "Protection. A reminder to watch over others." She drifted downward, tracing the elaborate edges of the anchor. "Symbol of the Navy. Represents strength and hope." Her fingers paused above his wrist. "A clock. To remind me time is short and shouldn't be wasted."

She moved to the other arm which held thick black lines in the tribal symbol. "For friendship?" she asked.

"Yes, this is my reminder of friendship and the strength of brotherhood." Rising above the simple sketch, an elaborate angel with wings outspread over his bicep floated in vivid color. He watched her face as she studied the ink. The look of wonder twisted his gut with need.

"An angel? For God?"

She swiveled her gaze and met his. He trailed a finger down her soft cheek, pressing his thumb against her swollen lower lip. "To remind me there's something bigger than me. And as much as I love control, I'm not really the one in charge in the end."

Her breath skipped. Those dark eyes widened, and suddenly, he was kissing her, but it was different from the other times. This time, his tongue stroked and seduced, drank in her honeyed sweetness with patience, savoring every slick movement of her mouth under his. Tenderness stirred. Warmth uncurled in his belly and heated his blood, and then he was hard and ready for her again.

He broke the kiss slowly, with reverence.

"Thank you, Leo."

His name fell from her lips in a symphony of sound. "For what, little one?"

Her sigh was pure pleasure and joy. "For helping me realize I was right about myself, and he was wrong."

He stiffened at the mention of her ex. He'd tried to make her feel ugly about who she was. If Leo had been able to show her she was beautiful inside and out, it was one of the most satisfying moments of his life.

"There's nothing wrong with wanting more from your sex life," he said, stroking her cheek. "You should never apologize for being who you are. There are men who will worship at your feet and fuck you senseless the way you deserve. Don't ever settle."

"I won't. But you managed to do something that will make all the difference."

"What's that?"

She tilted her chin up and smiled at him. His breath caught in his throat at that stunning, open smile meant just for him. "You made me feel beautiful again," she said softly.

Raw emotion slashed through him. This had never happened before. He was well known in the BDSM industry to love playing with a variety of subs and form no attachment. Leo always figured he'd been wired to be non-monogamous, or maybe never meant for a long term, exclusive relationship. He'd never experienced anything other than attraction, respect, and friendship. People told him they were building blocks to something greater, but for him, the spark never took flame.

Until right now.

An odd wash of fear froze him in place. He stared at her smiling face, at her wide Gypsy eyes and tumbled hair, her pale skin and red lips, and fell hard for a stranger he'd just met a few hours ago.

Refusing to hold back, he took the leap.

"I want to see you again," he said simply. "I know tonight is supposed to be anonymous, but I'm willing to change the rules. I want to remove my mask. Learn more about you. Take you to dinner. Bind you in my chains. Show you the world of BDSM—the world I find so beautiful and freeing and truthful. That's my new proposition, Scarlett."

Leo held his breath. He'd never been so off-balance. The need for her to agree; to want more like him; twisted inside. Ridiculous. He was a grown ass man and he finally understood how a boy feels asking a woman to prom. Worried the wrong answer will tear something permanently and he'll never be the same.

Her smile faded. Regret flashed briefly in her eyes, but then she pressed her cheek against his chest, as if trying to remind herself he was real. Her voice came out in a husky whisper. "I don't know if I'm ready for more. But I know something changed in me tonight. I know I'm not ready to leave you yet. I'd like to stay tonight, if you'll let me."

It wasn't the answer he wanted, but damned if he didn't respect her truth. He decided not to tell her about moving to Vegas at this point. She agreed to stay. He had till dawn to change her mind, and damned if he wasn't about to take on the challenge of a lifetime.

"Then you're mine until morning. And we are officially in a scene."

With one swift movement, he flipped her over and pushed her to her knees. She gasped, but didn't fight him. With her delectable ass high in the air, he quickly cuffed both wrists to the bed, then dragged her legs far apart. Her ass was still a rosy pink from her previous spanking, and her pussy was already wet with anticipation.

"Say it, Scarlett."

She trembled. "I'm yours till morning, Sir."

"That's right. I'm going to fuck you from behind now. Hard. You are not to make a sound. Not a whimper, or I'll make sure you don't come for the next hour."

Her breath hitched. He watched with satisfaction as her arousal dripped down her thigh. Oh, she was so delicious to play with. "Y-y-yes, Sir."

"If you do make a sound, I'll introduce you to a ball gag and we'll do this all over again, without the orgasms. Understood?"

"Yes, Sir."

He donned the condom. Sunk his dick deep into her sopping pussy, sputtering a curse as her tight channel squeezed him mercilessly. Then pounded into her giving flesh like a caged animal desperate for freedom, giving her everything he had, and damned if when she came, not a sound emitted from her lips, not a groan or a whisper, and Leo knew he'd do anything in his power for this night to never end.

But it did.

And in the morning, when he woke, she was gone.

Her black mask was the only thing left behind.

Chapter Six

LEO STARED AT HIS COUSINS and wondered if he'd heard wrong.

"You want to hook me up with an escort service? When I can walk into any club and get laid on my own terms and not pay?"

Rem gave a groan and rubbed his head. "I said the same thing when Rafe approached me, but I'm telling you, dude, it works. I found the love of my life again through the Fanta-C agency. It's not what you think."

"Wanna know what I think?" He leaned over and nailed each of his four cousins with a stare. He'd been in a piss poor mood lately and their ridiculous claims of fairy-tale, happy-ever-afters only made it worse. "I think you're all fucking crazy."

They sat in the Study—a quieter lounge to grab a drink, tucked in the back of the supper club in the Cosmopolitan Hotel. With comfortable leather chairs, dark wood, and bookshelves lining the walls, the lounge gave patrons the chance to take a breath, enjoy a well-crafted cocktail, and share a deeper conversation. The low strains of classic vinyl played on the speakers rather than the usual DJ or club music.

Rome laughed, hooking his ankle comfortably over his knee and tilted back his beer bottle. "We know how it sounds. But I called the number and now I'm with Sloane. It's worked for each of us." His premature grey pegged him as a George Clooney look-a-like and the oldest of the crew. But it was Rick who was the true leader of the Steele clan. His wife, Tara, affectionately called him Thor because of his long blonde hair and blue eyes. Of course, she was the only one he allowed to get away with it. Leo remembered when they were kids, he and Rafe were teasing Rick, calling his dick a limp hammer with no magical power.

Leo got a black eye, Rafe ran away, and Rick never got called Thor again.

Rick regarded him across the table with his narrowed gaze that saw too much. He was the quietest out of all of them, but had a laser like intensity and the ability to spot a lie, making him a perfect Dom. Of course, he was officially off the market and had never seemed happier.

Had Rick become one of these dudes who needed everyone else to be married because he was now content? Fuck. Now that he thought about it, all of his cousins were blissfully hooked up. Did they really believe an escort agency was responsible?

"You've been here three months and you haven't moved on from that masquerade party," Rick said. "You need to let it go."

Leo stiffened. "Maybe Jonathan and Cruz will get Hartley to tell me where she is."

Rafe, the last in the bunch, rolled his eyes. "She doesn't want to be found," he threw out with his usual starkness. Rafe's military background was evident in his cropped hair, deadly stillness, and the occasional shadows in his eyes. He'd had a rough time in Afghanistan, but he seemed softer now that he'd found his fiancée, Summer. He tipped back his shot glass of Jack Daniels. "You have to respect her wishes."

Familiar pain lurched in his gut. What was wrong with him? How had a woman he'd known for only a few hours gotten so deep under his skin? Sometimes, he'd catch the scent of citrus, and stop in his tracks. Last week, he could've sworn he saw a woman with long dark curls spilling down her back and launched through the casino to surprise a stranger. He was acting like a lovesick, schoolboy desperate for any contact. But Scarlett was long gone. When he'd asked his friends to track her down, they'd been sympathetic but firm. They weren't about to share her identity without her consent. Discarding her mask on the nightstand and disappearing before morning told Leo she didn't want to be found. Just like Rafe said.

Leo drained his whiskey. God, he was pathetic. Vegas suited him. From the moment he arrived, he embraced every gaudy, over-the-top detail that the strip offered. His security work at the casino challenged him, and he liked his team. Already, he'd made a bust and filled in some gaps that had previously urged card counters and cheaters to swarm in on the weekends. He loved the dry, strangling heat; the merge of day into night as time paused; and the pumping nightlife of the clubs and bars after hours. The city was alive, buzzing with potential and life. He realized being back with his cousins filled an empty place inside of him. They'd always been close growing up, and eventually all of them moved to Vegas to be card dealers. Since his mother had passed, he hadn't seen his father, and as an only child he craved being part of something bigger—the simple bond of blood and family. Was he going to spend the rest of his days grieving over something he'd never even had? There may have been the possibility of something there, but Scarlett made her own choice to leave him. For her, he'd only been a one-night stand. It was time to move on.

With resignation, he lifted his palm. Rem grinned and pressed a black and gold card into his hand. The word *FANTA-C* was scrawled across in embossed gold. On the back, a phone number was listed. "What do I do?"

"Call the number and use my name as your referral. Fill out your paperwork and if they find you a match, they'll set everything up," Rem said.

Rome cut in. "It's not guaranteed you'll get a match, and it's not always about sex. Just tell them what you really want. You have nothing to lose, dude."

They were right. He tucked the card in his pocket. His cousins shared a pointed glance, and Rem cleared his throat. "Umm, after you make the call you need to burn the card."

Leo lifted a brow. "You kidding me?"

Even Rick looked uncomfortable. "Just do it. Part of the rules."

"Then how'd you get your card?" he asked Rem.

"If they find you a match, they give you one card as your referral. You're mine."

This time, he couldn't help it. He burst into laughter, shaking his head. "I can't fucking believe it. You've all been bamboozled. You really think if you don't do these things something bad will happen?"

Rafe glared. "Don't give us any shit. It worked for all of us. We're trying to help your sorry ass. You've been moping around Vegas way too long about the girl who got away."

"She was a hell of a girl," he said quietly.

Rafe's face softened. "Not if she didn't think you were special."

All gazes swiveled to stare at Rafe. "That was poetic, bro," Rome said.

Rafe stuck up his middle finger and they all laughed.

Leo sipped his drink, falling into easy conversation about work and wondering why the card seemed to be burning a hole in his pocket.

Whatever. He had nothing more to lose. He'd make the call and put Scarlett Rose behind him as a beautiful memory.

***

Scarlett shook her sweaty palms in the air to dry them. *Gross.* Her heels clicked on the gleaming floor as she paced, staring at the door every few seconds. The hotel suite was luxurious and held a sensual vibe, but she didn't spot any special equipment or chains hanging from the ceiling. What if her date didn't show? What if this whole thing was just some lame joke? She hadn't been this nervous in a while, not since the night of the masquerade ball.

The memory stirred, along with her body. How many times had she woken up with his name on her lips? How often had she replayed their precious hours together while she brought herself to orgasm? When Hartley called and said Leo was desperate to track her down, she'd been overjoyed. Scarlett opened her mouth to tell her friend to give him her number, but when she pondered the consequences, she remained silent. It was better to keep her anonymity.

Her divorce chased her like a shadowed ghost, always a few steps behind. Her decision to leave Baltimore and move to Vegas was key in rebuilding her new life. For the first time, she stood on her own, and the power was a heady pill she greedily swallowed. When she thought of seeing Leo again, aching need mixed with a sinking fear she couldn't battle.

After only one night, she already felt attached. Connected. Her entire purpose was to free herself completely for the new adventure before her—not fall hard for another man. When he asked to see her again, she'd been desperate to say yes. But Leonardo Sinclair was a powerful man. His natural dominance and aching tenderness stirred something to life deep inside again, something she'd been missing for way too long. He'd shattered her completely and put her back together in a few short hours. How could she risk being involved in a new relationship so soon?

She just wasn't strong enough. Not yet.

So, she'd left her mask and Leo behind.

These past four months had shown her how much she'd grown. Her job as a statistician for the casino was challenging work, and she loved her new co-workers. Sure, she was spending most of her time at the job, but working with numbers and sorting through scenarios of how each fit into the real world defined an important part of who she was. Still, there was an emptiness inside that hadn't been filled since Leo. It was time to take another leap in her personal life and try to move forward. Calling the number on the business card her new friend had handed her seemed the perfect way to begin.

A soft knock vibrated on the door.

She dragged in a breath and smoothed down her form fitting skirt. Her date's requirements were exact. Black lycra tank top with a pencil skirt. Hair loose. Bare feet.

Red lipstick. No bra. No panties. Bare pussy.

She was ready.

Scarlett opened the door.

And came face to face with the man she couldn't forget.

hapter Seven

IT WAS HER.

Scarlett Rose.

He stared at her framed in the doorway and for the second time in his life, felt the ground shift beneath his feet. His silly heart leapt at the same time his mind snapped to attention and strangled the burst of hope. This couldn't be real. Was she playing a joke?

She may have been wearing a mask the last time he saw her, but she'd imprinted herself on his memory. The pale, smooth skin. The way her inky hair tumbled over her shoulder in riotous waves. The heavy dark brows arched over those cat eyes, framed by thick lashes. The sharp, clean scent of citrus. exposing the elegant lines of her face, finally exposed to his full view. Her patrician nose emphasized her high cheekbones and full lips, stained the same dark red as that night.

His gaze swept over her lush figure. She was dressed to his specifications and so fucking sexy, his dick stiffened and pushed against his jeans.

The skimpy tank emphasized her stiff nipples pressing against the cotton, and squeezed her breasts together in a gift offered only to him. The pencil skirt showed off her hour glass hips and curvy ass, just like he'd hoped. Her toes were painted cherry red and gave her the touch of vulnerability he relished in a submissive.

He realized in that moment he'd dressed his date imagining her being Scarlett.

He'd gotten his true fantasy.

Her gravelly voice matched the one in his dreams. "What are you doing here?"

It took a moment for him to gather his composure and realize she looked as shocked as he did. "I signed up with Fanta-C. I'm supposed to meet my date here."

She blinked and grabbed the doorway as if she was faint. "So, did I. Which means—"

"We're each other's dates," he finished.

He'd gotten his true fantasy.

He shook his head and tried to clear it. "What are you doing here?"

"I signed up with Fanta-C. I'm supposed to meet my date here."

Leo studied her closely, but she looked just as shell shocked as he did. "Me too. Which means—"

"We're each other's dates," she finished.

She stared back at him with open hunger, and he realized this was the first time she saw his face without a mask. Anger stirred in his gut, the reminder of her total rejection burning through his veins like acid. He beat back the hesitancy and walked through the door, forcing her to move aside. The click of the knob as he shut it echoed in the silence.

"Did you know it was going to be me?" he asked quietly.

"No! I-I had no idea. Though I did ask for specific details." Her cheeks burned. Had she done the same thing? Requested the agency set her up with someone exactly like him to re-enact their night together? "What are you doing in Vegas?"

He crossed his arms in front of his chest and regarded her. "I live here. Why aren't you in Baltimore?"

"I live here, too!"

The bigger meaning of her answer broke through him, and once again, hope spurted up. All this time she'd been right under his damn nose. Wild coincidence? Dumb luck? Or Fate?

His body didn't give a fuck. Already, his fingers itched to touch her, rip off those clothes, and shove deep inside her hot, wet pussy. But he needed to know the truth before he decided how the evening was going to be structured. "Then I guess neither of us could have planned tonight. I reached out to Jonathan and Cruz, you know. To see if I could contact you."

A flicker of regret crossed her face. "I know. Hartley told me."

Her answer ripped through him, driving the breath from his lungs. He struggled to maintain his calm expression and forced himself to ask the next question. "You didn't want me to find you again, did you?"

His razor-sharp gaze took in her pause. The seconds stretched and he waited to see if she'd try to lie to him. He almost wished she would, because he valued truth among all the virtues the most. But damned if she didn't tilt her chin up and say the cutting words.

"No."

He nodded, admiring her at the same time he took the hit.

"I wasn't ready for more than one night. I knew I was moving to Vegas and I wanted a clean slate."

"Fair enough." He made sure he sounded casual, even though his gut churned. Funny, the first time he falls hard for a woman and she had no intention of having more than one night of sex. If it wasn't so screwed up, he'd laugh in irony. "That leads to my final question. We both signed up for something tonight; something we wanted fulfilled. I need you tell me yours."

This time, she averted her gaze and began to turn. Oh, no, if they were going to do this, he was following the path all the way to the end, whether either of them liked it or not.

He snapped his voice like a whiplash. "Don't turn your back on me, Scarlett."

She froze. Her lower lip trembled, but she managed to square her shoulders and face him again. "I'm sorry, Sir."

The title knocked him back like a sucker punch. Damn her. He ignored his rapidly pounding heart and pushed on. "You will answer my question. What was your fantasy?"

Those inky eyes widened, filled with a churning mix of want and apology; of need and regret. "I wanted to feel like I did that night with you." Her voice broke. "Free. Powerful. Seen." A shudder wracked her body. "I can't go back to the way things were. Before…you. I need it again."

"You need the BDSM," he said in a clipped voice. "You need the feeling you get when you surrender."

"Yes."

"Have you visited another club? Been with another Dom since me?"

She shook her head, then caught his warning glance. "No, Sir. I joined the club Chains but I haven't played yet."

"Why not?"

"Because I've been afraid. Jonathan and Cruz introduced me to Blasphemy, but I don't know anyone here yet. I've been trying to get my nerve up."

His chest tightened. A hard, empty ball of ice lodged in his gut. Of course, she didn't want him. He could be anyone. It just so happened he gave her the first satisfying experience in the BDSM lifestyle, and she hadn't met anyone else.

She didn't miss him at all. Only his talent as a Dom.

The irony shred him to pieces. She'd haunted him for months, and now that she was finally in front of him, she only wanted him for the sex. The bond he'd believed they found had only existed on his side. His fantasy had been to find a woman just like her to fall in love with and claim forever.

Hers had been for more great sex.

He smothered the raw pain of rejection and studied her. Even now, her chin tilted up with a pride that was part of her, even as her body already seemed to soften in his nearness. Fine. He couldn't claim her heart, but damned if he wouldn't claim her sweet body and brand himself on her forever. She'd never be able to fuck another man without thinking of him. Never be able to submit to another without remembering what he alone could give her.

Shattering, mindless, blinding pleasure.

So be it.

"Do you remember your safe words?"

She jerked in surprise. "Yellow to slow down. Red to stop."

"This time, you will not forget to address me as Sir or your punishment will not be fun like the last time. You will not speak unless spoken to. Remove your clothes and stand in front of the window with your hands clasped behind your back, feet wide apart. We are officially in scene."

He began to unbutton his cuffs.

Chapter Eight

SCARLETT SWAYED SLIGHTLY, but kept her focus on the man before her to complete the task he'd given. Her body leapt to attention, greedy for everything he could do to her, but her heart squeezed with pain.

He was different this time. Cold. Distant. As if her words had ripped away the aching tenderness and left only the dominance. A lump rose in her throat but she'd been the one to make the rules. She'd left him. The flash of pain in his eyes seared her vision, and almost drove her to her knees. Dear God, she hadn't meant to hurt him. Now her actions seemed cruel—leaving him behind without a good-bye after the intimacy they'd shared.

Her gaze roved over him, greedy to savor every inch. He wore black pants and a formal white shirt with the collar unbuttoned. Slowly, deliberately, those talented fingers unbuttoned each cuff and he rolled up the sleeves, exposing the gorgeous ink on his muscled arms. His scent rose in the air, a heady combination of earth and spice, as primitive and sexual as the man. With his face uncovered, she noticed his nose had a slight bend, as if he it had once been broken. Stubble clung to his chiseled jaw and emphasized the fullness of his lower lip. His features were craggy and a bit rough, which only added to his sensuality. But it was his eyes that held her mesmerized; a swirl of smoke and ash; fire and ice; emanating a fierce energy that shimmered from his aura and pinned her helplessly in place.

He'd given her an order.

She needed to obey.

Her trembling hands tugged off her tank, and she had to wriggle the skirt down over her too wide hips with a little shimmy she prayed was halfway sexy. He watched her under heavy lidded eyes, then held out his hand. She gave him her clothes, then walked slowly to the window. A shiver bumped down her spine at the feel of the cool air over her bare skin, kissing her nipples and contrasting deliciously with her already heated pussy. She felt his gaze probing, sweeping over her nakedness, and she walked proudly, remembering his pointed lesson of believing in her own beauty.

She clasped her hands behind her back, parted her legs, raised her head, and lowered her gaze to the floor. Then waited.

Silence settled in the room. She stood patiently and had no idea how long had passed before the air stirred and his shoes appeared in her vision. Her nostrils flared when she caught his scent. Her skin pulled tight and she tried hard not to squirm as arousal throbbed in her core. The raw vulnerability as she stood before him, like a prized possession, thrilled her. Her busy mind slowed and her world began to shift, narrowing to this moment.

"I own your orgasms. I will tell you when to come and how many times. If you please me, you may get this." He stroked his cock, hard and long and tenting his pants. Her mouth watered. She'd never been overly enthusiastic about blow jobs, but the thought of her kneeling before him, her tongue stroking him to release, his rough hand guiding her to exactly how he liked to be pleasured--shuddered through her in raw, primeval need. As if he caught her thought, he made a murmur of approval and circled her like prey.

His hands stroked down her spine, cupping her ass, then dipped between her legs to spread her wide. His thumb played with her hard clit and his index finger sunk inside her, stretching deep, wresting a moan from her lips.

"You're very wet," he said in satisfaction. "Do you like being on display for me? Knowing I own every inch of this body—every wet, greedy hole and every strand of hair on your head belongs to me. Do you enjoy waiting to see how I'm going take you, with my tongue or fingers or my cock?"

"Yes, Sir."

He slipped out and began to probe her ass, his thumb playing with the tight hole where no man had ever been. Her muscles tightened, but he kept up the pressure, slipping into her up to his knuckle. A blast of pain melded with a strange, sinking sort of pleasure—a dirty, shameful heat flushing her skin. "Have you had someone take your ass?" he asked in a dark voice.

"No, Sir."

"It's better I prepare you for the next Dom. He'll want to take that pretty ass and own it."

Her mind rebelled at the thought of a stranger penetrating her there. She only wanted Leo to introduce that type of pleasure. But she kept quiet as he walked away. She heard the slide of a drawer, and then he returned to stand beside her. The squirt of a bottle cut through the air, and she shifted slightly.

A sharp slap vibrated against her ass. "You will stand completely still at all times."

"Yes, sir," she gasped. Tingles shot through her, but her mind was too distracted by what he was doing behind her. Oh, God, her ass probably looked huge from this angle, and if he made her bend over what if he thought—

Another slap shook her. She gasped at the sting.

"Do I need to demonstrate how I feel about this body, Scarlett? Or would you like another lesson?"

"N-no, Sir."

"Give me the words."

She closed her eyes but forced herself to say it. "My body is beautiful."

"That's correct. Now, I'm going to plug this beautiful ass and admire my handiwork. Bend over and grab your ankles. Then you're going to take three long, slow breaths."

"Yes, Sir."

He assisted her with a firm hand pressing her back down. Her mind fought the image of her ass stuck in the air, while a different type of heat uncurled inside, spreading out like licking flames. Something hard pushed through the ring of muscle, and she took another deep breath, trying to accept the invasion rather than fight it. He worked the plug back and forth, slowly and deliberately, and on the final breath, the muscles gave way and the plug sank all the way in.

"Very nice."

Oh, it was strange. Like something foreign had invaded her body, and didn't know whether to push it out or pull it in deeper. She wriggled slightly, and then he tapped the plug and vibrations spilled through her lower body. Oh, that felt good.

"Straighten up."

She did. He moved away again, and she heard the clank of metal scraped on metal. The opening and closing of a drawer. She desperately wanted to turn her head but knew that would gain her a punishment, and she was too excited to see what he'd do next.

When he came back, he held a spreader bar and two strips of black cloth. "It may get hard to keep your feet apart this whole time, so I shall give you some assistance." When she remained silent, he arched a brow in warning. "Did I hear a response?"

"Oh! Thank you, Sir."

He knelt in front of her and attached both ankles to the bar. Her legs were now spaced widely apart, her pussy on full display. "Ah, that's better. Now I can see those puffy, pink lips begging for me. Your needy little clit is hard already, little one. Do you ache?"

"Yes, Sir." Her words came on a breathy gasp.

"Very good. Let's get you a bit of help with your hands."

"Thank you, Sir."

He wrapped the soft cloth around her wrists, binding her arms so they lay against her lower back. He stepped back, studying her at his leisure, his finger tapping his lower lip in thought. "Beautiful. Almost done. We just need the blindfold."

Her eyes widened. "Blindfold, Sir?"

His voice hardened. "Is this a hard limit you didn't previously specify?"

"No, Sir."

"Good, then you have your safe word." He took the final cloth and covered her eyes, tying the knot behind her head. Darkness fell and surrounded her. Without her sight, her senses were more alert, ears pricked for sound, body bracing for the unknown.

"Are you ready?"

She swallowed. "Yes, Sir."

"Good. Just one simple thing." She stiffened, but already knew what was he was about to say. "Don't come."

She held back a tortured groan and swore she'd die before disobeying. "Yes, Sir."

"Very good, little one."

At first, Scarlett wondered if she was imagining the feather light touches over her body, skimming flesh as soft and faint as a butterfly's wing. The sensitive curve of her shoulder, the dip of her belly, the back of her knee, the hard tip of her nipple. It took a while for her mind to stop calculating the next touch, or sift through her churning thoughts, but as he kept bestowing touches on her starved skin, a quiet began to grow inside.

She softened, becoming fluid under his fingers, caught in the delicate web of sensation.

The air hissed. The thump of the flogger reached her ears right before the pain exploded on her ass. She jerked, moaning, then arched under the stinging heat as pain morphed into something more. He whispered in her ear, dirty things, beautiful things, kissed her nipples and licked them in apology. She arched for more of his wet, hot mouth, giving in.

The flogger blasted her again on her ass. Her thigh. Raining blows in quick succession that stopped almost as quickly as it started, leaving her a trembling mass of nerves and hurt and hot, throbbing need.

More whispers. Soft strokes over her belly, fingers diving into her pussy to rub and pluck and tease, urging her hips to rock against them in greed, arousal dripping from down her thighs, and then—

The flogger on her inner thigh.

She clenched and groaned, trying to close her legs, but his tongue was licking at her ear, biting her lobe, telling her she was perfect, and beautiful, and his good girl, and his fingers rubbed her skin, taking away the sting.

Until the flogger began again.

Caught in a world of heaven and hell, she began to beg, desperate to escape the flogger, desperate for more. The orgasm hovered, growing bigger, like a tsunami ready to break and shatter her into pieces.

The last lash ripped a scream from her lips. Her safe word hovered on her tongue, ready to be uttered.

Then he was licking her pussy and sucking her clit, his thumbs parting her swollen folds and fucked her with his hot tongue and dragged her back to the edge, where she hovered mercilessly, begging to fall.

"Sir? Please."

"Not yet." His fingers slipped around and played with the plug, twisting and moving it in and out in gentle motions. Sensation spilled through her, tightening the muscles in her belly and pelvis, adding to the ferociousness of her looming orgasm.

"Oh, God, please, please—" she begged brokenly, desperate, mad with need. He dragged his tongue over her throbbing clit and plunged three fingers deep into her pulsing channel. "Come."

She exploded. Tears streamed from her eyes as the brutal pleasure tore her apart, her body wildly bucking against him as he continued licking her, gripping under her thighs to tilt her up to his hungry mouth, keeping her from collapsing.

The fabric tugged around her bound hands, releasing them. Her world suddenly tilted, and she was lifted up in the air, then dropped onto a soft mattress on her back. His vicious growl raked across her ears, along with the sound of a zipper. Still shaking from her orgasm, her feet secure in the spreader bar, Scarlett waited, surrendering completely to everything and anything he wanted to do to her.

His thick cock pushed inside, and with one strong thrust, he was buried to the hilt. She gasped, unable to move, just allowed to take as he pounded in and out of her pussy with a violent need she embraced. She chanted his name and sunk into every sensation he forced upon her—the sting of the plug in her ass, the burning tightness of her pussy clenching around him, the ache in her thighs and arms, and the endless need choking her more…more…more…

He roared her name as he came, his fingers digging into her hips. She savored the slap of his thighs against hers and how his teeth sunk into her neck when he shuddered with his orgasm.

She lay on the bed, feeling like a broken ragdoll, well used. She felt him leave the bed and heard the rush of water in the bathroom. The spreader bar was released, and he rubbed both of her ankles, flexing her legs. With gentle motions, he flipped her over and urged her to kneel so he could slip the plug out. He disappeared again, and when he returned, the blindfold fell away from her eyes.

Scarlett blinked against the rush of light. Stared into his dark eyes. Then lifted her hand to stroke his rough cheek.

His voice was a low rasp, filled with aching tenderness. "Are you okay, little one?"

Tears stung her vision. She was empty and full at the same time. A tide of emotion rushed in, squeezing her insides, and she choked on the need to tell him she was wrong to leave him, wrong to think she could forget him, wrong to believe this wasn't more than one beautiful night. She only knew she'd die if the coldness came back into those eyes.

"Please don't leave me."

He bent forward and touched his forehead to hers. "No, sweet Scarlett. I'm not going anywhere."

He pulled her in tight against his chest. His heart beat steadily in her ear. The scent of sex, sweat, and musk filled her nostrils. Contentment unfurled, blooming like a neglected flower suddenly given water and light, and she gave in with a long sigh, closing her eyes and cherishing this man and what he had given her.

Chapter Nine

IT WAS HAPPENING AGAIN.

Leo held her close, stroking her back as she relaxed so trustingly against him. How could she incite such violent lust one moment, and heartbreaking gentleness the next? His one goal to concentrate only on sex had already crumbled under her wide, pleading eyes and trembling lips.

She'd already gone halfway into subspace and he'd only scratched the surface of where he could take her. The way she opened up and allowed him to push her edges; the beautiful way she surrendered under the flick of the flogger and stroke of his fingers, shattering around him with such truthfulness, he was almost driven to his knees.

This is what he'd always craved. A woman who could offer all these things.

But was it the sex or *him*? The BDSM experience or *him*?

"Leo?"

He pressed a kiss to the top of her head and pushed away his doubts. "Yes?"

"Where'd you get all that equipment from?"

He chuckled. "I had everything stored beforehand in the cabinets. Do you really think I'm an unprepared Dom?"

He felt her smile against his chest. "No. I guess I was expecting you to bring a bag like a doctor."

"I like keeping my submissives off balance."

Her nails curled into his shoulder. "Do you have many submissives?"

He'd never try to make her jealous. Honesty was everything to him, and another reason he loved BDSM. The communication between partners was key to the intimacy. "No, Scarlett. I've played with various partners throughout the years but haven't had a serious relationship in a while. I was traveling with the Navy for a number of years, and became kind of a wanderer, always looking for new places to settle. I haven't been tempted to change my lifestyle for a woman yet."

She seemed to absorb his answer, her mind clicking to sort through the information like a good little statistician. He'd always had a weakness for math nerds, especially ones laying naked and satisfied in his arms. "Is it wrong that I'm glad there's no one else?"

"No, it's honest. But you did walk away. I wanted more. You didn't."

She lifted her head and met his gaze. Those inky eyes pulled him deep, trapping him with the strength of her emotion. "I made a mistake," she said simply. "I thought it was for the best. I was wrong."

His muscles tightened. He grabbed the back of her head, fisting his fingers in her hair, and yanked back. Her lips parted, damp and red and inviting. Like the poison apple? Or the fruit that could nourish his body and soul?

"Tell me why," he demanded.

"After my divorce, I felt as if I was trapped in my old life. Baltimore was full of memories of my ex and who I'd become, and I wanted a fresh start. That night at Blasphemy, I promised I'd allow myself to let go and give myself one perfect memory before I moved away. I wasn't looking for a deep connection, or a relationship, or anything that would deter me from something I needed to do. Wearing a mask allowed me to surrender."

He nodded. God knows, he understood needing something for yourself. "Did you feel like you never had that opportunity because of your marriage?"

"Yes. I married young, and I fell into a routine that I never questioned. I worked in a small office from nine to five and went home to cook dinner. I drank one glass of wine per night for good heart health but not two because it made me tipsy. Peter and I would spend a quiet evening together, or go out with a few couples from his job. Then we'd have missionary sex every Friday night. Maybe take the occasional vacation, snapping selfies to post on Facebook so everyone knew I was happy." Her voice caught, but she shook her head and continued. "I was dying inside. Trapped in a life that on the surface seemed perfect, but always craving more. After I left him, I began therapy and finding myself again. But that night, when I met you, I was terrified of *not* leaving. I had a new job lined up in Vegas, with an apartment and a blank canvas I got to fill. If I said yes, I may have stayed in Baltimore. If I said yes to you, I felt like I was saying no to me."

Her words tore through him. Naked vulnerability carved out the lines of her beautiful face, but she confronted him with her chin held high and determination glittering in her eyes.

"What's changed now, Scarlett? It's only four months later. What's different from the last time?"

She dragged in a breath. "I realize I am strong enough to enter into a relationship without losing myself. That I'm a beautiful woman, that my needs aren't abnormal. You accepted me, as is. You embraced my sexuality, nurtured it. Since I left, I can't stop thinking about you. Dreaming about you. And now that you're here, I want to give us a chance for more. I need you, Leo, so much."

He groaned and stamped his mouth over hers.

Her honeyed sweetness filled him up as his tongue stroked and pleasured the wet cave of her mouth. He breathed in the clean, sharp scent of citrus, holding her tight as he plundered her mouth, desperate for everything. She kissed him back, looping her arms around his neck, giving it all back to him.

He pulled away and tipped her chin up, forcing her to meet his gaze. Frustration curled the edges of his voice. "You like the way I make you feel. I don't necessarily think it has to do with me specifically. You haven't been with any other Doms, little one. How do you know it's not the experience of surrender you're craving and not me?"

"Because it isn't." Stubbornness radiated from her form. "There's a connection between us. Bigger than just the sex or the BDSM. It's in your very touch, and your eyes when you look at me, and the way you can be cruel yet so tender my very soul stirs. No other man has ever given me that."

She was killing him. He fisted his hands, torn between his need to believe her and the raging doubt that told him she was still too inexperienced. But he couldn't walk away either. For now, he intended to spend the night learning everything he could in order to imprint himself on not only her body, but her mind.

"I want to know more of you. Beyond my chains and dominance." He pressed his palm over her naked breast, against her beating heart. "Open up to me tonight and give us a chance to take this out of the bedroom. If that's what you truly want."

"It is." He kissed her long and deep, sealing her promise. When he lifted his head, she was smiling up at him, her dark eyes joyous and lit with mischief. "What do you want to know?"

He grinned back. "Right now? Tell me—what you want to eat. I'm starving."

Her laugh charmed him. "French fries. With mustard and ketchup."

He wrinkled his nose. "Ugh, that makes no sense. You need to choose."

"Why? I want it all."

He tapped the bridge of her nose. "Then you shall have it." He cocked his head in sudden deliberation. "Fries or onion rings?"

"Fries."

"Coffee or tea?"

She rolled her eyes. "Coffee. Duh."

"Thank God. I could never trust a tea person. Dogs or cats?"

"Dogs."

"Another good answer. Morning or night person?"

"I'm practically a vampire," she said.

His gaze dropped to the vulnerable curve of her neck. "Hot vampire fantasies?"

"Maybe."

The flicker of interest in her eyes told him definitely. Damned if it wouldn't be fun to bite and ravish her. "I think we'll get along just fine," he drawled, pleased her skin was flushed just from his voice. He loved the way she responded to him— making him feel like a fucking superhero.

Leo called in the order to room service and shrugged on his pants. She devoured him with her gaze, sitting cross legged on the bed. "Okay, now it's my turn," she declared. "You said you worked in security. Do you work in a casino?"

"Yes, but I'm not a security guard. I bust the people who try to cheat the casinos."

Her eyes grew wide. "Like in the mobster movies?"

"Less exciting. I don't send anyone out to break their knee caps." She looked so disappointed he chuckled. "I'm also a math nerd. Grew up being able to do complicated math in my head, and when I was in my twenties, I made a bundle counting cards. Until I got busted."

"Did anyone break *your* kneecaps?"

He arched a brow. "I had no idea you were so bloodthirsty. It's turning me on." He enjoyed her giggle and continued. "No, they were so impressed they hired me in Atlantic City. My cousins worked there for years—they're all poker dealers. But after a while I got itchy and joined the Navy. When I got home, I found my cousins had moved out to Vegas and hooked me up with a job. I missed them, and felt ready to settle back down so I drove out here."

"How many cousins do you have?"

"Four. Rick, Rome, Rafe, and Rem."

She blinked. "You gotta be kidding me."

Leo grinned. "Nope, they get tortured all the time. Aunt Alice named them each after a leading man she had a crush on."

Scarlett propped her elbows on her knees and leaned forward. "Oh, this I have to know."

He ticked them off his fingers one by one. "Rick Springfield. Roman from the soap opera, *Days of Our Lives*. Rafael Nadal, the famous tennis player. And Remington Steele—the TV show where the main guy was played by Pierce Brosnan."

Her mouth dropped open. "Damn, I wish I could meet their mother. She's cool."

He joined her back on the bed. "Aunt Alice is very cool."

"Is she your aunt on your mom or dad's side?"

"My mother, but I lost her a few years ago. Cancer."

She reached out and grabbed his hand. The simple gesture of warmth and comfort touched him. "I'm so sorry."

He smiled at her. "It's okay, little one. I came to terms with it. My father and I were never close, so that's another reason I wanted to move to Vegas. I missed being with family."

"I'd love to meet your cousins one day." She ducked her head with a touch of shyness. "I don't have any other siblings either. I'm close to my parents but they're in New York so I don't see them as much. I always wanted to be part of a big family."

"You want kids one day?"

Her smile lit up her face. "Oh, yes. At least four. Peter wanted to wait, but now I'm glad we did. It's heartbreaking to begin a family with the wrong person."

"Yes, it is."

Their gazes met and locked. The air between them shimmered with the usual energy, and he raised her hand to his lips, kissing her knuckles. Why did it feel so natural between them? As if they'd known each other much longer than two brief nights?

But could he really trust what they had? What if her feelings were mixed up with the natural high of submitting to an experienced Dominant? He prided himself on sensing what a woman needed from him. Leo needed that punch of satisfaction and power of being that type of Dominant. He knew Scarlett meant more to him than just a physical encounter. But how could she really trust her instincts without allowing herself to broaden her experiences?

The discreet knock on the door interrupted his thoughts. "I'll be right back." He dropped her hand and turned, trying to ignore his churning gut and the inner voice that told him he might have to leave her in order to truly know if she was meant to belong to him.

Chapter Ten

SOMETHING WAS WRONG.

They'd eaten fries, split a hamburger, and argued over the proper condiments to put on all food. He'd regaled her with stories about growing up with his cousins, even admitting Rafe still held the scar from their brilliant game of chucking rocks at each other in a deadly, updated game of hide and go seek.

Boys.

She relished every grin and hungry gaze. Reveled in the occasional touches as he ate, and the sizzling heat that crackled between them like a live wire. But Scarlett noticed a slight frown to his brow, as if a specific thought was bothering him. She was determined to put him at ease. She'd already made her decision.

This would not be her last night with Leonardo Sinclair.

She wanted more. Wanted dinner and dating. Wanted to meet his cousins. Wanted to spend endless nights in his arms, learning about the beautiful world of BDSM. Wanted him as her Dominant, for herself.

Why wasn't she afraid any longer? Now that she was unmasked, with her heart open, there was no longer any fear or doubts. For the first time, she felt truly free to be her true self with him.

It was an incredible gift she intended to treasure.

She watched him get up from the table and prowl across the room. He reminded her of a graceful predator, all hard muscles and lean strength, from his abs to his pecs to that glorious ass. He stared out the window, jaw clenched with tension.

"What's the matter, Leo?" she asked softly. "Did I do something?"

"No. Not you. Me." She tilted her head, listening, and he went on. "I don't think you're ready for a commitment right now."

Her heart sped up. Her belly tumbled with nerves. "But I explained how I feel. Is it because you can't forgive me for leaving you?"

He turned to face her, shaking his head. "No, little one. I completely understand why you left. I have a responsibility to protect you and look out for your interests. It's part of what I love about being a dominant. And though we've shared something extraordinary, I think you need to experiment more before you can make the right decision about us."

She got up from the chair, pulling the edges of his shirt around her. "I already know what I want. You. Us. This. I have no need to play with anyone else."

Arrogance shimmered from his aura, along with a set determination that squeezed her heart. "I disagree. I'd be doing both of us a disservice if I didn't push you to explore this lifestyle and everything it can give you. As you said, you're just spreading your wings. You need to be sure."

"I am sure."

"I'm sorry. Chains is a good club. I can introduce you to some dominants who may be a good match to play with."

Anger mixed with desperation, bubbled up from inside and spilled out. "You can't make all the rules between us," she shot back hotly. "I can make my own decisions, Leo, and I choose you."

His lips tightened, and those dark eyes flashed with warning. "I will make the decisions I feel are right for you. Do you think this is easy on me? But it's the only way to see if this is real."

"No, it's not." Desperate to make him see, she gave in to her instincts and stripped off her shirt. His gaze focused on her nipples, already hard and needy. The fabric fell to the floor, and she stood proudly in front of him, owning her beauty and power and sexuality in a way she'd never done before. "Because I already know how I feel about you, and it's not temporary. It's not going away under the lash of another dominant's whip." She dropped to her knees, keeping her head up so he could see every expression on her face. "I ache for you, Leo, for what only you can give me."

And then she began to crawl toward him.

He sucked in his breath. His gaze devoured her whole, eyes lit with a fierce lust and need that burned her alive. The cool marble tiles were hard on her knees as she crawled across the room, stopping at his feet. His face was a tortured mask of emotions as he stared down at her.

"Scarlett?"

"Let me serve you. Let me show you what you mean to me."

His groan ripped through the air. She raised her palms upward in supplication, waiting for his command.

Heart-stopping seconds passed as he seemed to struggle with his inner demons. Then with a vicious curse, he ripped down his pants and exposed his erection, the tip already dripping with pre-cum.

"Suck me," he commanded.

She opened her mouth and took him deep.

Blow jobs had never been a highlight for her, but the moment she caught his musky taste, ran her tongue over the silky iron hardness of his dick, she was lost. She attacked him with more fervor than finesse, relishing every grunt and groan that escaped his lips. His fingers twisted in her hair and guided her head, forcing her to open her throat deep to take his full length, and she hummed with pleasure, feeling used and cherished and powerful.

He fucked her mouth and she took it all, her own arousal dripping down her thighs, her fingers working his balls as she squeezed and rubbed and sucked harder and harder.

And then he was coming, and he was yelling her name and she took it all, desperate to please him and own him like he did her.

He dragged her up, lifted her into his arms, and brought her back to the bed. She writhed and begged and pleaded under the wicked lash of his tongue, the bite of his teeth, and the hot touch of his skin. He took his time, worshipping every inch of her body, and then he donned the condom and pushed inside her.

He fucked her slow, forcing her to meet his gaze the entire time, drinking in every cry and gasp from her lips, every shudder from her body. And when she came, he watched her with animal satisfaction, owning her orgasm the way he owned everything else.

When they collapsed into each other's arms, Scarlett slept with a smile resting on her lips.

Until she woke up and he was gone.

***

"Wait a minute. You dissed her? The woman you've been moping over for the past few months? The woman you've been desperate to find again?"

Leo scowled at Rem over his coffee. The noisy sounds of chatter and plates crashing at the popular breakfast buffet distracted him from his sudden desire to rip into his cousin. "I didn't diss her. I left a note."

Rem whistled and sat back in the booth. "Dude, you fucked up."

He let out an irritated breath and tamped down on the sudden uneasiness twisting his gut. "You're not listening to me. I'm doing what's best for her. She needs to figure out if her feelings are for me or if they're just the physical high of being dominated."

"I know, you explained that. But she was clear that's not what she wanted. I know sometimes we make decisions on what we think is best for our subs, but she doesn't sound confused to me."

Leo forked up his eggs and regarded his cousin with determination. "I need to know for sure."

Rem nodded. "Okay. But she'll take it as a complete rejection. A retaliation for her leaving you."

"No, I was clear in my note why I left."

An amused chuckle escaped his cousin's lips. "Have you never been in a serious relationship? Women see things differently. What we think is black and white, females declare bluish, purplish grey. What did the note exactly say?"

"I told her she was special, and the night meant everything to me, but it was important for her to explore more of the BDSM world before she could commit to me in a relationship. I told her I'd set her up with someone at Chains."

"Yeah, I was right."

"About what?"

"You fucked up. Hell, not only did you reject her, you offered to whore her out to a friend."

"No, I didn't!" He dropped the fork and glared. Did he? Had he made a horrible mistake in his quest to do the right thing? "I want her to be safe and be sure because once she's mine, I'm not letting anyone else touch her."

"There. That's what you should've said to her, not like in your jacked-up note."

Ah, fuck. Maybe Rem was right. The idea of hurting Scarlett ripped at his insides. He had to track her down and talk to her. Leo pushed his coffee and plate away. "Do you understand why I'm not ready to trust her feelings for me? Or am I fucked up thinking that way?"

Rem's face reflected a shred of sympathy. "Nah, I get it. I'd feel the same. But first you gotta tell her how much she means to you so she doesn't think you're just pushing her away. Make sense?"

"Yeah. How'd you get so damn sensitive?"

He gave a suffering sigh. "Cara made me see things in a different light. Oh, clear your calendar for next weekend. I'm going to ask her to marry me, and I want all of us to go out and celebrate."

Leo grinned. "That's awesome. Congrats, you deserve it."

"Thanks. It feels good."

"I'm going to find Scarlett and fix this." He threw down his napkin and fished out his wallet.

Rem waved his hand in the air. "I got this. Just tell me one thing."

"Sure."

"Fanta-C worked, didn't it?"

Leo stilled. Frowned. Now that he'd thought of it, how the hell had an agency been able to hook him up with the one woman he couldn't forget, but left behind? A shiver shot down his spine. "Yeah. I guess it did."

Rem nodded solemnly. "Kind of spooky. Better be careful who you give your referral to."

He thought of the card at home on his desk. Hmm. He'd have to save it for something big. But for now, there was just one thing on his mind.

Talk to Scarlett.

Chapter Eleven

"SCARLETT! OPEN THE DOOR, I know you're in there. We need to talk."

Scarlett pondered the closed door with a fierce frown. Oh, she was pissed. And hurt, and betrayed, and…pissed. After waking up from the most wonderful night of her life, she'd rolled over to find a note pinned to her pillow, and an empty bed.

"I don't want to talk to you!" she yelled through the door. "You made your feelings perfectly clear in writing."

An irritated, masculine sigh came from the other side. "I fucked up. I'm sorry. I need to talk to you, Scarlett, please open the door."

She shifted on her feet at the softening of his tone. Cursing herself for being an idiot, she couldn't help twisting the knob and letting him in. It had only been twenty-four hours and already she ached for him.

She was such a goner.

He stepped inside. Dressed in jeans and white t-shirt, his dark hair was tousled, and stubble hugged the chiseled line of his jaw. He smelled of cotton coffee and sunshine. Scarlett curled her fingers into fists to keep from touching him, her body already melting inside her clothes.

Instead, she crossed her arms in front of her chest and gave him a challenging stare. "You left."

He winced and kept his distance. "I know. I thought my note explained things."

"For a man who believes in honesty and communication, that was a low move." She shifted her weight, hating to admit her next words. "You hurt me."

He groaned. Misery etched his features. "I'm sorry, little one. I truly am. I never meant to hurt you— I'm trying to look out for you. Protect you from making a mistake."

She studied him for a while, then shook her head. "No. You're trying to protect yourself because you don't trust my feelings for you."

He jerked back. Those dark eyes filled with anguish, and though she ached to go to him, she didn't move. They needed to follow the conversation through.

"Maybe you're right. Maybe what's happening between us is too fast."

She tried to mask the pain and touch of panic at the thought of losing him so soon after finding him. Such crazy irony. First, she left him. Then, he left her. They kept circling each other, unable to meet. Scarlett just had to find a way to forge both paths into one. "I'm ready to explore with you," she said softly. "But you have to trust me to know what I need. To trust who I need."

He closed the distance between them, sliding his hands around her back to tangle in her hair. His breath rushed warm over her lips, and she greedily drank in the sight and scent of him. "I want you to be mine, Scarlett," he growled against her lips. "But I don't want to scare you. I'm a possessive, greedy, demanding man, and it won't be easy to walk away from me." His warning rang with all the masculine power that made her belly drop to her toes. "I understand why you left me the night of the masquerade. You were finally free—and not ready to commit so soon. And I can take this slow between us, but I need you to be sure of what you want."

"How do I prove that to you?" She shook with frustration. "What do you want me to do?"

Determination gleamed in his eyes. "I've had years to explore this world, but you haven't. You should have all your options available. Go to Chains. Take some time and play with another Dom."

She stilled. "You want me to scene with another man?"

"I want you to explore more of the BDSM world with an experienced dominant I trust. My cousin Rem is a master there, and can help take care of the whole thing. I want you to take the time to really see if our night was real—or if you bonded to me because I was the one to take you into your first real scenes."

She wanted to shake him. Cry. Stomp her foot and throw an old-fashioned female tantrum. Rip off her clothes and kneel at his feet. But Scarlett knew in that moment there was only one way to prove to him her feelings were real. Even if it meant submitting to someone else. "You really need me to do this?" she asked softly.

Stubbornness threaded through his words. "Yes. For the both of us."

She closed her eyes. Dragged in a breath. And gave him her answer. "Then I will. I'll remove my clothes and give myself over to another Dom. I'll keep an open mind to the experience."

He nodded. "I'll set everything up for next Saturday."

"Will you stay with me for a while?"

He didn't respond. He kissed her, with an agonizing sweetness that stole her breath and her heart. When he lifted his head, torment gleamed from his eyes. "I can't, little one. I have to stay away from you so you can have an open mind. We both need the time apart."

"And what if I like it? Being with someone else?" she challenged.

His gaze was steady on hers. "I'll accept it. And I won't walk away because there's nothing wrong with having another Dominant helping you enjoy pleasure. But you'll also be sure if you want just me, or if it's too soon. You may need others for a while. And I'll know I wasn't the one to trap you by using the very thing that was able to free you."

With his taste lingering on her lips, he turned and walked out.

Scarlett stared at the door for a long time. God, how was she going to do this? She didn't want to play with another man. She only wanted Leo, but he didn't believe her.

She needed to talk to someone.

Scarlett grabbed her phone and dialed Hartley. Her cheery voice poured over the line. "Hey, I've been waiting to hear from you. How are you doing?"

And then it happened.

She burst into tears.

"Oh, my God! Scarlett, are you okay? Are you hurt?"

"No! I'm just being emotional, I'm sorry. I just miss you."

"I miss you too! Listen, I can get in my car right now and drive over."

Scarlett swiped at her eyes and laughed. "Sure. It's only a forty-hour drive."

"So, I'll get on a plane. I need a vacation anyway."

Her heart filled. Hartley was such a good friend; the miles didn't matter. "Thanks, Hart. I appreciate it. I think I need some advice."

"Tell me everything."

She did. She told her about meeting Leo again and her feelings and how she left him the night of the masquerade party even though she'd already been developing a connection with him. Once she spilled out the whole story, she felt a bit lighter. There was nothing like a girlfriend who had your back.

Finally, she stopped talking and took a deep breath. Hartley stayed silent for a while, probably trying to sift through the complicated tale.

"Here's my first question," Hartley said. "Do you want me to get Jonathan and Cruz to beat some sense into him?"

Scarlett laughed. "No. I'd like Leo to realize we're meant to be together on his own."

"Then you need to do what he asks. And not for Leo, sweetie. For yourself."

She froze with dread. "You don't believe me either?"

"No, silly! I know you're crazy about him and playing with another dominant won't change anything. But Leo sounds like the protective type. Even though it's screwed up, he's trying to do this grand gesture of letting you go to make sure you're happy. You went through hell with your ex, Scarlett. And now you finally have this brand-new life in Vegas, and Leo's probably terrified of scaring you off. He wants to love you, not trap you."

"I can see how he'd think like that," she said slowly. "You're saying I should go along with his suggestion?"

"I do. This will prove to both of you it's more than just sex. It's the connection you feel with him. The emotions. The…need."

"Hmm, sounds like you're experiencing those same things. How's it going with Jonathan and Cruz?"

Her friend's sigh was filled with content. "Really, really good."

Her heart swelled. "I'm so happy, Hart. You deserve everything, and those men are the ones to give it to you."

"Of course, it's not always easy. It can get complicated."

"They're men, Hart. Men are always complicated."

They laughed, staying on the phone for a while to catch up. When she finally said good-bye, Scarlett knew what she had to do.

For both of them.

Chapter Twelve

LEO STARED THROUGH THE two-way pane of glass and hoped he wouldn't crash through it.

A primal, possessive roar pumped through his blood and hovered on explosion. Watching Scarlett in her band aid skirt and a simple black lace bra that emphasized those lush curves was pure torture. The moment she stepped into the club to meet Master Evan, he'd been ready to call the whole thing off. But she had a right to have choices. Leo couldn't live with himself if he trapped her into a relationship with him because she didn't know her other options.

"You doing okay?"

He turned toward Rem with a growl. "No."

His cousin clapped him on the shoulder in guy comfort. "Sorry, I know it's hard. But I made sure she met with Master Evan so he got an idea of what she's looking for."

"He's single, huh?"

A gleam of sympathy shone from Rem's blue eyes. "Yeah. That's the only way this can work. If there's a connection, better you know now rather than later."

"And he's the best?"

"One of the best, yes. Evan is known to push the majority of subs into subspace. He's one of the most popular masters at Chains."

"Fucking fantabulous."

Rem smothered his smile. "They've discussed the scene in length so she's in good hands. Sure, you don't want to sit this one out? I'll be honest with you and explain everything if you want to go home."

"Hell, no. I'm watching every second. It's the only way I can be close to her."

The room reminded him of the one they'd played in at Blasphemy. Simple, functional, yet decorated with sensual colors and fabrics. There was a spanking bench, St Andrews cross, and a king size bed with various bondage equipment hooked to the posts. A large shaded window took up the right wall since it was themed for voyeurism. Leo ignored the comfortable chairs and sofas set up and propped his elbows up on the high counter so he could keep a sharp gaze on every detail of the scene.

As long as he didn't look at the bed.

It may kill him.

Master Evan approached her, and even Leo had to admit the guy was impressive looking. His blonde hair was caught at the nape of his neck, and even through the glass Leo caught the way his blue eyes pierced with a perceptiveness that pegged him as an experienced Dom. He was taller than Leo, his body more whip like and lean.

He watched Scarlett's face for her reaction to her new master of the evening, but she seemed calm, all her emotions tucked behind a smooth façade. If Evan did his job, that surface would shatter and break, allowing them both to glimpse the real stuff.

Master Evan studied her with hard eyes, taking it all in. "Please kneel."

"Yes, Sir." She sank to her knees, gaze lowered, knees apart. She still wore the skirt and bra. Her feet were bare.

"Very good. You may stand and remove your clothes, fold and hand to me."

Her hesitation was slight, but she rose and slipped out of her skirt, then unhooked her bra. As she stood before her new Dom, Leo had to fight not to close his eyes against the sudden need to go to her. Break up the session and take over. She was so fucking beautiful, naked and vulnerable and standing tall, with her shoulders back, pride glowing on her face as she owned her sexuality.

"You're very beautiful," Master Evan said, taking her clothes. "Please stand against the wall and face me. You will lift your arms high over your head and spread your feet wide."

"Yes, Sir."

She obeyed, and Master Evan pulled down the chains from the ceiling, buckling her into the cuffs and adjusting the fit. The room was small enough that Leo could spot every detail. Goose bumps peppered her arms. Her nipples were hard. Her belly quivered. But when she spread her legs wide, he didn't see her usual dampness, and her inner thighs were dry.

Master Evan cuffed her ankles, then stood back. "Perfect. I want you to breathe, Scarlett. Inhale deeply, hold for a moment, then slowly exhale."

"Yes, Sir."

She breathed, her heavy breasts lifting like a gift, and Master Evan began touching her. His fingers stroked and explored, rubbed and teased, urging her to let go into the sensations of her body while she breathed. He lowered his head to suck on her nipples, manipulating her the exact way Leo knew she loved. His dick pushed against his jeans, desperate for relief, and he sank into a terrible pit of lust and anguish, adoring her open submission the same time his soul wept that she was being touched by another.

Master Evan murmured something in her ear the same time his hand slid between her legs, his fingers slipping inside her.

Leo groaned. His breath strangled in his lungs.

Master Evan stepped back. A slight frown creased his brow, and he seemed to change up his game. He walked to the bureau and withdrew a feather, a flogger, and a brush with sharp spikes.

Sensation play.

"I want you to close your eyes, Scarlett. Keep them closed until I tell you open them."

"Yes, Sir."

He began to slowly bring her body into the full swing of the scene. Leo admired his flawless technique. The master knew exactly when to back off from the edge of pain and into pleasure, from the whip of the flogger, to the slow tease of the feather, and the rub of the prickly brush strapped to his hand. And the whole time he watched her body jerk and move under Master Evan's toys, her breath coming a bit faster, and the flush to her pale skin.

Caught between heaven and hell, Leo watched it all, and Master Evan once again slid his hand between her legs.

"Open your eyes," Master Evan commanded.

Leo's breath stopped as Scarlett stared back.

Tears shone in those inky depths, along with a deep sorrow that ripped through him. Her lips trembled. Her voice broke. "I'm sorry, Sir."

Master Evan dropped the flogger, his hands cupping her cheeks with concern. "Scarlett, why didn't you use your safe word if you were uncomfortable?"

She shook her head. "It's not that, Sir. Everything you did was fine. I liked it all. But you're not the man I want and I can't pretend."

Leo placed his palms on the glass. His world tilted, then righted itself in perfect harmony. His entire being stilled.

Scarlett didn't want any other Master but him. She had no idea he was here tonight, watching the scene. The raw honesty of her reaction to Master Evan told him what he needed to know.

He wasn't about to waste another minute.

Leo pulled away from the window and walked toward the room.

***

It was all wrong.

She stared up at Master Evan in sheer misery. He was sexually attractive, kind, and was able to coax her body to slight arousal, but inside, she remained untouched. She'd enjoyed their dialogue together and found him interesting and intelligent. He was the perfect package.

But he wasn't Leo.

Master Evan stroked her cheek. "Why don't I get you out of these bonds and we'll talk?"

"You may leave my submissive as is, Master Evan."

Scarlett jerked in the chains. Her mouth fell open as Leo strode into the room with his usual arrogance and power. Master Evan regarded him, glancing back and forth between them for a few moments, then stepped back, letting his hand drop from her cheek.

"Leonardo. I didn't realize you were here tonight. Or that this was your submissive."

"Let's just say I was waiting to make the perfect entrance." The man who held her heart swiveled his gaze to stare at her with command. "Scarlett, tell Master Evan who I am."

A smile of pure joy curved her lips. "He's my true master."

"Then you may be needing this." Master Evan handed Leo the flogger, and slid off the glove. The feather had already drifted to the ground.

"Thank you. I appreciate you warming up my sub."

"It was my pleasure. She's a beauty." With a nod of respect, Master Evan left the room.

Her heart thundered as Leo slowly walked toward her. "You were here the whole time?" she asked.

"I had to know." His face held regret but a new resolve she hadn't spotted before. "And now that I do, the rules are about to change."

A thrill shot through her. That dark, dirty voice poured over her body and between her thighs, leaving her wet and aching. "Yes, Sir."

"You belong to me. No more play with other doms."

His hands stroked her face, down her shoulders, over her breasts. She melted into him. "Yes, Sir."

"No more leaving before morning for either of us."

Her trailed kisses down her neck; sunk his teeth into her shoulder. His thumb flicked the hard nub of her nipple back and forth. His knee pressed between her legs, giving her just enough pressure on her clit to drive her mad. "Yes, Sir."

"You're all mine, Scarlett Rose. And I'm never going to let you forget it."

His fingers drove inside of her with merciless intensity. She cried out his name as her hips arched up for more, but he kept up his own rhythm as his mouth claimed hers, his tongue plunging between her lips to mirror his fingers. Ruthlessly, he twisted and rubbed her clit with his thumb, forcing her on her toes, trying to fight the bonds that held her to get closer. He laughed with satisfaction, playing her like a fine instrument, and then she was coming, jerking against him in abandon. He nibbled on her lip, soothing her swollen flesh, and then her drowsy gaze met his.

"What do you say to me?"

She shuddered at his demand and gave him the words they both needed.

"Thank you, Master."

He smiled and pressed his forehead against hers. "Very nice. Now, let's further your education since we have this room for the whole night."

Scarlett smiled back and knew this time; the gift of her heart would be well taken care of.

The End

Author's Note

I hope you enjoyed this newest installment of the Steele Brother Series. Please make sure you subscribe to my newsletter. I never overwhelm your inbox, and offer exclusive giveaways and new material to subscribers.

http://www.jenniferprobst.com/newsletter

I'm thrilled to announce *Reveal Me* is part of a Special Cross-Over Release with Laura Kaye's *Theirs to Take* from her Blasphemy Series! If you want to know more about Hartley, Jonathan, and Cruz, you can read their story here:

Buy at Amazon!:

https://www.amazon.com/Theirs-Take-Blasphemy-Laura-Kaye-ebook/dp/B073SY7LGT/

Subscribe to Laura Kaye's newsletter!

http://www.subscribepage.com/x7t8e0

Other books by Laura Kaye:
Hard to Serve:
https://www.amazon.com/gp/product/B018FCU0SG/
Bound to Submit:
https://www.amazon.com/gp/product/B01H2KDTEE
/
Mastering Her Senses:
https://www.amazon.com/gp/product/B06W597M4
W/
Eyes on You:
https://www.amazon.com/gp/product/B01M4RR2JA/

Want to read about Rick, Rome, Rafe, and
Remington? Pick up the rest of the series here!

THE STEELE BROTHER SERIES
Catch Me...
Rick Steele has avoided relationships since he caught
his fiancée cheating, but when his friend refers him
to the exclusive agency, FANTA-C to experience the
night of his dreams, he's not prepared for his
emotional and physical reaction to his date. Tara
shows him a raw passion and honesty he's never
encountered. For the first time, Rick wants more than
one night, but he needs to catch her first...

Tara Denton escaped a brutal past and needs one
night with a stranger to get beyond her sexual and
emotional limitations. On the brink of recovering her
strength and independence, she wants nothing to do

with a relationship. But Rick Steele does more than rock her body…he rocks her heart. Tara has to make a choice, but is she ready to get caught?

Amazon

Play Me…

Professional gambler Sloane Keller is tired of dating weak willed men and longs to meet a man who challenges her dominant personality and forces her to submit. As the Queen of Cards, she's used to making her own rules and craves the excitement of Vegas. But her inner heart cries out for someone who can be her match, both inside the casino and in the bedroom.

As the new dealer in town, Roman Steele is burnt out on women looking for a quick penny and a man to follow. He craves a woman with fire in her soul and a keen intellect who can challenge him. When his brother recommends the exclusive agency, FANTA-C to give him one perfect night, Rome is amazed at the complicated woman who challenges both his body and soul. But when the evening is over, will she be gutsy enough to offer him forever?

Amazon

Dare Me…

As a military leader back from the war, and the youngest of his two dominant older brothers, Rafe Steele struggles with a secret. He craves surrender in the bedroom under the controlled hands of a Dominatrix. When his brothers offer him an experience through the exclusive agency, FANTA-C, he jumps at the chance to experience one perfect night. After one experiment, he's sure he'll be able to move on. But he never counted on Summer Preston to strip down his walls and make him want more so much more...

An elementary school teacher with a girl next door, fresh face, Summer is constantly barraged by men who want to take care of her, but she longs to meet a strong man who can handle her dominant ways in the bedroom. Trapped in her own storybook life, she books a one-night stand to finally experience her fantasy. But she never counted on Rafe Steele to push her boundaries in both the bedroom...and her heart.

Amazon

Beg Me...

Remington Steele comes to Vegas to be with his brothers and try to get over the one woman he's never been able to forget. As childhood sweethearts, she hadn't been able to handle his Dominant tendencies, choosing to run away without a good-bye. But when he's suddenly face to face with Cara Winters, all grown up and finally ready to be his, Remington needs to make his own choice. To leave the past behind forever, or forgive and be with the woman he's always loved?

Cara wasn't ready to be the type of woman Remington needed in his life, so she disappeared and broke his heart. But she's changed, and is ready to embrace the woman she always craved to be. She begs him to take her for one night, and Remington finally agrees. Will they get a second chance at love, or are the scars from their past too deep to heal?

Amazon

THE BLASPHEMY SERIES

12 Masters. Infinite Fantasies.
Welcome to the Erotic Romance Stand-Alones of Blasphemy...
Will insert all of Laura's buy links from amazon here:
HARD TO SERVE
BOUND TO SUBMIT
MASTERING HER SENSES
EYES ON YOU
THEIRS TO TAKE

Enjoy the first chapter from Laura Kaye's *Theirs to Take*!

HARTLEY FARREN STARED at the wreck of her catamaran and tried not to cry. Or scream. Or punch something with her bare fist.

She'd done everything right to prepare for the hurricane that had come through the area two days before. Lighthouse Point's marina provided an excellent safe harbor with a fantastic track record of low storm damage, and she'd been sure to use long dock lines to allow the boat to rise and fall during the storm surge. But none of that mattered when someone else wasn't as diligent in his preparations. And the consequence had been that another boat had lost its mooring and the wind had driven it into her *Far 'n Away*, damaging the port side.

"I'm really sorry," the other owner said for the dozenth time. "I told Charlie we needed more lines, but he said the Chesapeake never gets hit that badly." In her sixties and sweet as pie, the lady made it hard for Hartley to stay mad when she revealed that their own boat, a total loss, had been their only residence for the past eighteen months, leaving them essentially homeless. They stood and watched while the lady's husband worked with the harbor master to have the wreck towed away.

"I know," Hartley said. "It'll all work out somehow. For both of us."

Hartley had to believe that. Because that cat was her whole life.

Her father had left his chartering business to her when he died three years before. Now, that business and that boat provided her whole income and allowed her to keep her grandmother, who suffered from Alzheimer's, in a lovely assisted-living community.

But now Hartley was dead in the water. Or, at least, her chartering business was. Until she dealt with the insurance claims and found someone to do the repairs. Both were sure to be a pain in the butt following a big storm.

Hartley sighed. Neither crying, screaming, nor punching something was going to make anything better. And she'd certainly fared better than some others—she had to be grateful for that. She slid the business card detailing the couple's contact information into her pocket and said her good-byes, and then she made her way to the marina office.

"Hi Linda," she said to the office manager she'd met for the first time when she was only eight or nine. Back then, Hartley had been her dad's "first mate" as much as going to school and playing field hockey had allowed.

"How bad is it, hon?" Linda tucked the gray hair of her bob behind her ears as she came around her desk. The office was a big square with four desks, the back two partially hidden behind cubicle partitions. Normally, the room was bright and airy, as windows lined the two exterior walls, but boards currently covered the glass, making it feel like nighttime in the middle of the day.

"Fixable. That's not the problem, though. The problem is whether it can be fixed fast. There's no avoiding having to cancel several weeks of charters, but I'll be sunk if I have to pull out of the Sailboat Show and the Sailing University courses I'm teaching." Thank God, she'd been smart enough to buy business interruption insurance, but that was only going to cover her so far. If she didn't get the *Far 'n Away* repaired within three weeks, well, she wasn't going to think about that. Not yet.

"What can I do to help?" Linda asked, giving her the same affectionate, grandmotherly look she'd been giving her for the past twenty-plus years. It was an affection born not only from their long-time friendship, but from the fact that Linda and her father had been close—close enough that Hartley suspected something romantic between them before her dad unexpectedly died of a heart attack. Since then, Linda had been one of the few people who seemed to understand the grief and loneliness Hartley had been working through.

"Can I borrow a desk and your Wi-Fi?" Hartley gestured to the messenger bag on her shoulder. "I have my laptop and I'd love to dive into finding a place that can do the work."

"That's easy. Of course. You know your way around. Make yourself at home."

"Thanks, Linda. What would I do without you?" she asked as she sat at the more private desk behind Linda's.

The older lady peered around the corner at her and smirked. "Says the woman who spends days and days alone at sea. You'd get by just fine. You don't *need* me, Hartley. I'm just your cheerleading section."

Hartley chuckled. "Well, I appreciate that, too." She set up and turned on her laptop. She'd just looked up the contact information for her insurance company when Linda returned and placed a steaming mug on the desk.

"I'm also your deliverer of mint tea." Linda winked.

And clearly also a goddess," Hartley said, taking the cup in hand. She adored the feeling of warm ceramic against her palms. "Can't forget that one."

"Naturally," Linda said. "Hey, since you're here, can you let anyone who comes know I'll be right back? I have to run over to the Harbor Master's office for a short meeting."

"You got it," Hartley said, sipping at the sweet, minty tea. A moment later, the front door opened and closed, leaving Hartley alone to figure out who was going to be her savior.

Scheduling a time to meet with the insurance adjuster turned out to be easy enough. But, thirty minutes later, she'd called a dozen boat repair shops and only found two willing to consider the work—but neither could even come look at the cat for almost a week, nor commit to completing the repairs within the next three.

Hartley dropped her head into her hands and heaved a deep breath. In the quiet, the soft opening and closing of the outer door reached her ears. "Hey, Linda," she called. Then, to herself, "What am I going to do?"

"Hey, are you okay?"

The voice was deep, male, and definitely not Linda's. Hartley's gaze whipped up. And up. To find a tall and incredibly sexy man standing in the doorway to her cubicle. Sun-kissed shoulder-length blond hair framed a ruggedly masculine face and intense gray eyes that were at once inquisitive and observing. Broad shoulders and defined muscles pulled taut a heather-gray T-shirt with a single word written across the chest: *NAVY*. His forearms and legs beneath a pair of khaki cargo shorts were toned and tanned, as if he spent a lot of time in the sun.

"Uh, hi. Yes. Sorry. I'm kinda in my own world here. Did you need Linda?" Hartley managed as she pushed to her feet. At five-five, she wasn't short, but his impressive height made her tilt her head back to meet his assessing gaze.

117

He shook his head. "I was coming by to see if she needed any help around the marina."

"Oh. Wow. I'm sure she'd appreciate that. She stepped out to a meeting but she should be back soon if you'd like to wait." Despite his selfless reason for being there, the man made Hartley nervous. She wasn't sure why. Maybe it was the intensity behind those odd, gray eyes. Or the way he towered over her. Or how freaking good-looking he was.

"I'll do that. Thanks."

"Sure," she said. But he didn't leave. "Um, anything else I can do for you?"

His gaze stayed glued to hers, but she had the oddest feeling that he was checking her out nonetheless. He smiled and shook his head. And, *man*, was his smile a stunner, highlighting the strong angles of his jaw and charming her with the way the right side of his mouth lifted higher than the left. He thumbed over his shoulder. "I'll just grab a seat."

And then he disappeared from her little doorway.

Hartley was half tempted to peer around the corner and watch him walk away. Just to see if the rear view was as impressive as the front.

On a sigh, she dropped back into her chair. And even though her thoughts should've returned to the huge problem of fixing her boat, they lingered on the Good Samaritan currently making small noises on the other side of the room. Who was he? Hartley had essentially grown up around this marina. Even though she couldn't say she knew everyone here, she still recognized most of the regulars. And she'd never seen Mr. Tall, Blond, and Ruggedly Handsome before.

Her cell phone buzzed, pulling her from her thoughts.

"Hello?" she answered.

"Mrs. Farren, this is Ed Stark returning your call from Stark Restoration."

Hope rushed through Hartley. "Hi, Mr. Stark. Thanks for calling back so quickly. And, please, call me Hartley." Being called 'missus' was almost laughable when she couldn't remember the last time she'd gone on a date. With rebuilding the business after her father's death and taking care of her grandmother, Hartley didn't have time to date. Or, at least, she hadn't made the time. Not that she'd had any prospects motivating her to do so. Shaking the thoughts away, she filled the man in on the damage and the challenge of her timeline.

"I might be able to get someone out to take a look at your boat by the end of the week, but you're at least the tenth call I've had today. I wouldn't be able to guarantee a completion date without assessing the damage, and I've got a number of other repair jobs ahead of yours at this point."

It was the same thing all the others had told her. And she got it. She did. It wasn't anyone else's problem that she depended on the *Far 'n Away* for her livelihood. Or that she'd put most of what her father left her into her grandmother's home and a bigger boat that could carry more passengers two years ago. Or that July had been so rainy that her normal charter business had been halved. Or that she needed the extra income that the sailboat show and Sailing University courses would bring in to make it through the leaner winter months.

Just then, the front door opened again. "Hartley, I'm back. Sorry I was gone so long." This time, it was definitely Linda. "Oh, Jonathan. How are you? How did you guys make out in the storm?"

"Our shop's fine, ma'am," the man said. "Thanks for asking." Jonathan. Jonathan who apparently had a shop somewhere in the marina?

Even more curious about him, Hartley stepped out of her cubicle and tried not to stare. Or drool. She forced her gaze to her friend. "Hey, Linda. Everything go okay?"

"Oh, yes. Just little fires everywhere that need put out," Linda said, dropping a legal pad full of notes onto her desk. "Were you able to find anyone to do the work?"

Hartley's shoulders fell. "No. No one can even look before Friday." And with a hole in the side of the cat, who knew how much more damage it might sustain over those four days.

Linda frowned, and then her gaze swung to Jonathan. "Have you two met yet?"

That intense gray-eyed gaze landed on Hartley, unleashing a whirl of butterflies in her belly. "Haven't had the pleasure to do so officially," Jonathan said.

It was a simple statement. But something about the word *pleasure* from that man's mouth made a tingle run down her spine. It'd clearly been too long since she'd been on a date. Or been kissed. And waaaay too long since she'd last had sex. Embarrassingly long. Like, she didn't even want to admit to herself how long.

(Fifteen months.)

With that fantastic thought in mind, all Hartley managed to say was, "Uh, hi. Again." She chuckled to cover how much she wanted to duck back into the cubicle and bang her head against the desk.

He grinned. "Hi. Again. I'm Jonathan Allen."

"Hartley Farren." Feeling Linda's amused gaze on her, she cleared her throat. "You have a shop in the marine center?"

He nodded. "A&R Builds and Restoration."

"Jonathan and his partner Cruz own the business that moved into the old Stanton space at the beginning of the summer," Linda added helpfully.

Hartley's eyes went wide as her heart kicked into a sprint. "*You* do builds and restoration?"

He chuckled. "As the name suggests."

She didn't even mind the teasing, not when he might be able to help her. "Then you might be my new favorite person."

"Is that, right?"

The office phone rang, and Linda excused herself to answer it.

Hartley stepped closer to Jonathan. Why did that make her feel like she was approaching a usually friendly but sometimes lethal animal? Her stomach did a little flip. "Yes, because I need a huge, huge, *gigantic* favor."

He arched a sexy brow. "And if I do this favor, will I *officially* be your favorite person?"

She grinned, enjoying his playfulness—and the fact that he was entertaining doing her a favor when they barely knew each other. "Without question. I'll even make you a certificate. *Jonathan Allen. Hartley Farren's Favorite Person.*"

That crooked smile emerged again, and hope flooded through her. "Hmm. I don't know. I mean, a certificate is nice and all, but..."

Was he playing with her? She thought he was, but she didn't know him well enough to know for sure. Hartley braced her hands on her hips. "Are you teasing me? Because that would be evil, Jonathan, and you don't strike me as an evil man." Now *she* arched a brow.

His chuckle this time was different. Deeper. Grittier. Sexier. With an undercurrent of...something she didn't understand. "You never know, Hartley."

Her stomach did a little flip, because it had been eons since anyone had flirted with her. Let alone a man this attractive. "Oh, come on. Can I at least tell you what my favor is?" she asked.

Those gray eyes sparkled with amusement. "Well, I couldn't help but overhear your phone conversation, so I might have an inkling."

Wait. He *knew* what she needed and still hadn't said no? Hope and anticipation rushed through her, making her feel restless and brave. "Then if my awesome certificate idea isn't enough, what can I offer to convince you to walk out to my slip and take a look at my catamaran?"

That eyebrow arched again, and Hartley suddenly felt like they'd been playing chess—and her words had just allowed him to put her in checkmate. But still, he didn't make any claims of her.

She stepped closer and dared to flirt back. "Jonathan. Mr. Allen. *Mr. Allen, My Already Officially Favorite Person*, are you going to make me beg? Because that wouldn't be very nice," she added playfully.

Those gray eyes flared. She would've sworn they did. He bit back a chuckle as he shook his head. And when his words came, they were filled with a deep intensity that made her shiver. "Why don't you show me your boat, Hartley, and then I'll answer your questions."

About the Author

Jennifer Probst wrote her first book at twelve years old. She bound it in a folder, read it to her classmates, and hasn't stopped writing since. She took a short hiatus to get married, get pregnant, buy a house, get pregnant again, pursue a master's in English Literature, and rescue two shelter dogs. Now she is writing again.

She makes her home in Upstate New York with the whole crew. Her sons keep her active, stressed, joyous, and sad her house will never be truly clean.

She is the New York Times, USA Today, and Wall Street Journal bestselling author of sexy and erotic contemporary romance. She was thrilled her book, The Marriage Bargain, was ranked #6 on Amazon's Best Books for 2012, and spent 26 weeks on the New York Times. Her work has been translated in over a dozen countries, sold over a million copies, and was dubbed a "romance phenom" by Kirkus Reviews. She is also a proud 3 time RITA finalist.

She loves hearing from readers. Visit her website for updates on new releases and her street team at www.jenniferprobst.com.

Sign up for her newsletter at www.jenniferprobst.com/newsletter for a chance to win a gift card each month and receive exclusive material and giveaways.

Jennifer's Playlist

Get Low – Zedd & Liam Payne
Feels – Calvin Harris feat Pharrell Williams, Katy Perry
Slow Hands – Niall Horan
No Promises – Cheat Codes featuring Demi Lovato
Ain't No Rest for the Wicked – Cage the Elephant
Feel It Still – Portugal, The Man
Body like a Back Road – Sam Hunt
Say You Won't Let Go – James Arthur
Feels Like Tonight – Daughtry
Let's Hurt Tonight – OneRepublic
Cheap Thrills – Sia featuring Sean Paul
This is It – Michael Jackson